A TENDER CONFLICT

Believing a local meadow to be the site of an ancient battle, Kristin Lacey and her small band of eco-protesters set up camp there in order to fend off ruthless property developer Daniel Hunter and his plans for 'executive' homes. Then Kristin discovers her mother has a secret that could put a spanner in the works — and, to make matters worse, she finds herself increasingly attracted to the very man who should be her enemy. When her feelings betray her, is she playing straight into his hands?

SUSAN UDY

A TENDER CONFLICT

Complete and Unabridged

LINFORD
Leicester

First published in Great Britain in 2014

First Linford Edition
published 2015

A catalogue record for this book is available
from the British Library.

ISBN 978–1–4448–2589–3

Published by
F. A. Thorpe (Publishing)
Anstey, Leicestershire

Set by Words & Graphics Ltd.
Anstey, Leicestershire
Printed and bound in Great Britain by
T. J. International Ltd., Padstow, Cornwall

This book is printed on acid-free paper

1

Kristin Lacey stared at the two men standing in the middle of the meadow, their heads close together as they studied a large sheet of paper. She was on her way home for the first time in three months but had decided to make a detour and take a look at the twenty-acre field that would soon be no more. Instead, it would be a development of 'executive homes', as Hunter Associates described them; the cheapest would be a million pounds to buy. And there they were, the potential vandals — or, at least, their representatives. They certainly weren't local men; she was sure she'd recognise them if they were, despite her absence from the village over the past months. And, let's face it, why else would they be standing in the field with what looked suspiciously like a set of plans in their hands?

It was simply too good an opportunity to miss. If her own hands had been free she would have been rubbing them.

Instead, she pulled her rather elderly Fiesta off the road and through the open gateway, and parked it alongside a very smart Range Rover before turning off the engine and climbing out. She noticed one of the men swivel his head to look her way. She tightened her lips. He and his friend were about to get a very large piece of her mind. See how they'd like that. Not stopping to consider the wisdom of what she was about to do — alone, she climbed from the car and started off across the grass.

The other man now also turned to stare at her. Neither moved nor spoke as she strode towards them. Her bearing, she hoped, was one of resolve and determination; so it was rather unfortunate that, within feet of reaching them, her one foot should encounter an unexpected dip in the grass. She staggered forwards, tripped, and only just managed to save herself from an undignified fall. As it was, she lost a shoe in the process.

She heard a muffled gasp and then one of them was there, holding her by the arm, steadying her and asking, 'Are you okay?' She glanced up into a pair of eyes that were such a light shade of grey they bordered on silver; they were also glittering with what looked dangerously like amusement.

'Yes, thank you.' She rammed her foot back into her shoe. So he found it funny, did he — that she'd nearly fallen flat? She yanked her arm from his grasp. She certainly didn't need any further help from him. 'I presume you're from the company who are about to start building houses here?' Her glance flicked towards the large sheet of paper in his hands.

He nodded. 'Ye-es.' He was watching her intently now, the silvery gaze darkening as his eyes narrowed.

'You do realise that there's every possibility that this could be an ancient battle site? A battle site that you plan to destroy in order to build yet more million-pound *executive* — ' She sarcastically emphasized the word. ' — homes. Historic artefacts have been found — '

'Very insignificant artefacts, I believe,' he murmured, 'and the possibility of it being a battle site has been more or less discounted.'

'Oh, has it?' she blazed. 'By whom? According to the local paper that's not what the experts say. They believe it could have some sort of connection to the Wars of the Roses.'

'Experts? You mean the local historical society? You don't want to listen to that pack of tree-huggers,' the other man snorted. 'And some sort of connection? Far too vague to hold up construction work.'

Kristin glared in his direction. Irritatingly, his response was a bold grin and a narrowing of his whisky-coloured eyes as they proceeded to rake her from head to foot.

She swung back to face the first man

she'd spoken to, only to discover that he too was scrutinising her, his gaze lingering on her violet eyes before moving to her freckle-dusted nose, her flushed cheeks, her shoulder-length mahogany hair, her parted lips. He even, finally, had the audacity to glance down, his eyes following curves that were only hinted at beneath her loose-fitting shirt. His gaze then returned to her face and rested on a mouth that was still compressed with anger.

Kristin felt her cheeks burn. She knew she looked a bit of a mess, but what was the point of dressing up when you were an eco-protester and had been living in a tent for the past nine months? Even so, she couldn't stop herself from glancing down to see that several buttons on her shirt had come undone, exposing rather more cleavage than she would have liked. It must have happened when she tripped. Hastily, and with cheeks that were turning a deeper red by the second, she fastened them up again.

'Oh, shame, I was enjoying the view.' It was the other man speaking, the one who had disparagingly described the historical society as a pack of tree-huggers. 'And,' he added, tilting his head to one side and scrutinising her every bit as closely as the first man had, 'I must say, I do like a woman with a bit of spirit.'

'I'm sorry you feel so strongly about this, Ms — ?' It was the original speaker again. She ignored the implied question — he didn't need to know her name. 'But the plans have been passed — '

'Yes,' she interrupted, 'but that was before the artefacts were found — a couple of weeks ago, as I understand it.'

It was as if she hadn't spoken, however, because almost without pause he went on, 'Mainly because the local community wants this development.' He looked completely unconcerned by her argument as well as her refusal to tell him who she was, and that simply intensified her irritation.

'Who told you that?'

'Everyone did, at a public meeting in which we quite clearly outlined our plans. In their view, it will bring money into the area, money badly needed at the present time.'

'Money,' she scoffed. 'That's all people like you think about. How much will you make in profit from this?' She waved a hand, indicating the entire breadth of the meadow. 'One million, two . . . ten?'

'I'm hardly likely to tell you that,' he said. 'But I will tell you that we have the authority to go ahead. The local council are as firmly behind us as the local people are.'

'I'm sure they are,' she snorted disparagingly. 'Gutless to a wimp, the lot of them. Another load of . . . of money-grubbers.'

His expression hardened. 'Maybe you should speak to some of the villagers before you rubbish the plans, and their integrity, quite so vehemently.'

Kristin turned away in disgust. She

was wasting her time with these two, and they most likely didn't have the power to change anything anyway. By the way they were dressed, in jeans and shirts, she guessed they were nothing more than employees. But the members of the council — how could they allow such destruction of a site that could be a valuable part of the nation's heritage? Or had a bit of bribery and corruption gone on? She wouldn't be surprised. She'd heard one or two rumours over the years. Just as she'd heard that the head honcho of Hunter Associates, Grant Hunter, was capable of almost anything, short of murder, to get his own way and make as much money as he could. Hateful man! If she ever met him . . . well, he'd get a massive chunk of her mind as well.

Her resolve strengthened as she strode away. He wasn't going to be allowed to do it. She'd joined a group of campaigners a little over nine months ago in an attempt to prevent exactly this sort of destruction. Now, she and the small band she'd persuaded to leave the main group and come here were determined about that.

For all that though, and despite her spirited show of defiance, Kristin's drive home was somewhat shaky. She suspected the two men had been quietly laughing at her. Well, they'd soon be laughing out the other side of their greedy capitalist faces. Her co-protesters would be arriving tomorrow and it wouldn't take them long to set up camp. They were well practised and had managed it in a day when necessary. She just hoped there would be enough of them to provide effective opposition. She'd noted the easy access via the gateway for their vehicles, mostly vans, but they'd very quickly dig a trench once they were all in, thereby preventing entry for any larger vehicles.

There were some trees in the field — not many, but they would almost certainly be felled before construction work began; they would provide one means of protest. Chains would be secured around their trunks to stop the chainsaws, and shelters would be erected in the branches for some of the more hardy campaigners. It was all designed to make felling them impossible. There would also be tents erected in the field. Sadly, they couldn't dig tunnels as they told her they often did, in case precious artefacts were destroyed.

Kristin's mother, Eve, had no idea that her daughter was returning home, just as she had no idea of Kristin's intentions once she got there. That was the bit that Kristin was nervous about. Eve heartily disapproved of the activities that her daughter had recently become involved in, and she'd made no secret of that disapproval — bemoaning every time Kristin either returned for a flying visit or, as she did more often than not, phoned her, 'I can't believe that a daughter of mine is consorting with such people, living in trees, waving banners. Whatever your father would say, I can't imagine. I'm almost glad he died when he did, because seeing you living this way would have surely killed him.'

Kristin neared the house and saw, to her dismay, a very expensive-looking Jaguar car filling the narrow driveway. Her mother had visitors. And here was her only child, dressed in a shabby shirt and equally shabby jeans. She could already see her mother's horrified expression and hear her words — 'For heaven's sake, Kristin, do you have to look as well as live like a tramp?'

Kristin parked in the road and heaved on the hand brake before grasping both her bag and a large bouquet of flowers and climbing from the vehicle. She then made her way to the pristine navy-blue door which was, as usual, flanked by pots of brightly coloured petunias and trailing geraniums. Pulling her house key from the back pocket of her jeans, she fitted it into the lock and pushed the door open. Almost at once she heard her mother laughing and then the deep tones of a man's voice. The sounds were coming from the sitting room at the rear of the house.

Belatedly, she acknowledged that she should have rung ahead and warned her mother of her impending arrival. But she'd so wanted to surprise her, and Eve loved surprises. Kristin had hoped it would go some way towards cushioning the blow of why she was really there.

'Mum,' she called as she deposited her bag onto the polished parquet floor of the hallway. 'It's me.'

'Wh-what?' she heard her mother gasp.

The man's voice rumbled, 'Who — ?'

'Ssh,' Eve hissed. 'Kristin, is that you?'

'Yeah. Tah-dah — surprise.' She walked into the sitting room, arms spread wide with flowers held aloft in greeting, to be faced with the sight of her mother and the man sitting extremely close together on the settee, hands clasped and both looking more than a little disconcerted, Eve especially. Her cheeks were prettily pink and her eyes were shining. And neither was due to the makeup that was adorning her face in rather more generous amounts than was customary. In fact Eve, Kristin noticed, was looking extremely glamorous — more glamorous than she'd seen her in the six years since her husband had so unexpectedly died. Her honey-blonde hair had obviously been highlighted and was attractively arranged, framing her heart-shaped face. She was dressed in a sleekly fitting jade-green dress that emphasised the fact that she had retained the figure that Kristin had inherited from her: full-breasted, with a neat waist and nicely rounded hips. A perfect 38-24-36 shape, in other words. A pair of well-shaped legs completed the picture. Not that you could see much of that in her case, Kristin reflected, camouflaged as it all was beneath her well-worn jeans and slightly-too-large shirt. Although the men in the meadow seemed to have had no trouble, as she recalled, if the warmth of their gazes had been any sort of guide.

Quickly, self-consciously even, Eve pulled her hands free and said slightly breathlessly, 'What are you doing here, darling?' It was clear, however, from her expression — one of dread, almost — that she'd guessed her daughter's reasons for returning home so unexpectedly. She refrained from putting her suspicion into words, however. Although, as if fearing what Kristin was about to blurt out, she did rush on to say, 'Um . . . ' She glanced at the man by the side of her. 'This is Grant, Grant Hunter.' The final two words were accompanied by a glare of warning at her daughter. 'And this is my daughter, Kristin.'

But Kristin couldn't help herself; she gasped, 'Grant Hunter? Not the Grant Hunter of Hunter Associates?'

'The very one,' the man said, the ease

of his smile a sure-fire indication that he was oblivious to Kristin's expression of horror. 'And I'm extremely pleased to meet you at last.'

2

To Kristin's disgust, she found herself taking Grant Hunter's outstretched hand as he went on, 'I've heard all about you.'

'Strangely, I've heard nothing at all about you; at least, not from my mother,' Kristin muttered. She couldn't believe that she was actually shaking this man's hand.

'Well, we don't speak that often, do we, darling?' Eve bit out.

Kristin decided not to respond to that snippet of criticism, mainly because she guiltily conceded that her mother had a valid point. They didn't speak often enough, mainly because each time they did, Kristin was subjected to recrimination and blame. Eve couldn't seem to understand Kristin's compulsion to try and do something to prevent the relentless

16

urbanisation of the nation's country-side, to somehow protect it from the likes of Grant Hunter. To do some-thing worthwhile, in fact; and maybe, in some small way, make her mark on this world. And it wouldn't be forever, for heaven's sake. Kristin had been clear about that from the start. At some point, for financial reasons if nothing else, she'd need to get back to work.

In an attempt to avert a possible row now, she asked, 'So, how did you two meet? I don't imagine you mix in the same circles.'

'Well, there you're wrong,' Eve snapped for the second time. 'I'm not quite the unsophisticated country mouse you obviously think I am.' It was evident that Eve was more than a little flustered, not to say exasperated, by her daughter's unheralded arrival.

Grant Hunter, for his part, had remained silent throughout this exchange. Although, with that last little jibe of Eve's, his mouth did begin to twitch as amusement danced within his eyes.

Kristin slanted a glance at him and rather grudgingly conceded that he was extremely good-looking, with hair that had greyed at the temples yet retained its rich chestnut colour over the remainder of his head. He had strikingly blue eyes, an aquiline nose, and a very determined-looking chin. He was also tall — six foot one or so, she estimated — and well built. She could see why women would be attracted to him, but — and despite what appearances seemed to suggest — surely her mother and he weren't an item? A man more dissimilar to her father she couldn't imagine.

Eve went on, more calmly now, 'I met Grant at a friend's house a couple of months ago.' She smiled at him before directing an ever-so-slightly-smug glance at her daughter. 'I was asked to dinner at Grayling House. You know the place, a couple of miles out of the village?'

Kristin nodded. It was the local

manor house, owned by the Grayling family for centuries. They'd originally made their money in Elizabethan times — huge amounts, apparently, which subsequent generations, it was rumoured, had frittered away.

'Do you remember the Bellamys?' Eve now asked. Kristin again nodded. 'Well, the Graylings were finally forced to sell — there'd been some unfortunate stock market dealing, so I heard — and the Bellamys bought it for a knock-down price. He — Greg, that is — did extremely well with some investments, apparently. That was, let me see . . . six, seven months ago. They're good friends of Maureen and George.'

'The Crispins?'

'Yes. They were a woman short, so Maureen suggested me . . . ' Her words tailed off beneath her daughter's quizzical gaze. 'And yes, to save you the embarrassment of asking — Grant and I have — ' She glanced at Grant then, as if seeking reassurance. ' — been seeing each other ever since.'

Grant reclaimed her hand at that and lifted it to his lips. Eve made no attempt to free it this time. Instead, she smiled gratefully at him, squeezing his fingers.

'Even though he's hell-bent on destroying a valuable historic site; our environment, even?' Kristin burst out; she simply couldn't stop herself. Mainly because she couldn't believe her mother was seeing such a man.

'Don't exaggerate.' Eve gave a light laugh. 'He won't destroy the environment. It's just a few houses.'

'Oh, really? Just a few houses — on an ancient battlefield? And it's not just that. It'll also mean wealthy nimbies moving in, virtually on your doorstep. They'll then proceed to complain about everything, from muddy lanes at harvest time to cocks crowing in the mornings. Oh, and let's not forget the cacophony of the church bells on a Sunday morning, ruining their precious lie-ins. I've heard it all so many times.'

'Well, I'm sorry you don't approve,

Kristin,' Eve retorted, 'but that's how it is. Grant and I are . . . very fond of each other. Anyway, changing the subject, are you here to stay?'

Conceding defeat in the argument for the moment at least, and struggling to match her mother's evenness of tone, Kristin said, 'I thought I would for a while, if that's okay?' Belatedly, she wasn't at all sure it would be. With Grant so prominently in the picture, her mother might not want her around, intruding on what was obviously a very cosy twosome.

'Well, good heavens, of course,' Eve quickly said. 'It is your home — when you remember you have one, that is.' This last was said with undisguised irony. But then, as if Eve finally felt guilty for her blunt words, she hurried on to say, 'And it will give you the chance to get to know Grant; really know him. It's also quite fortuitous, because I'm having a little dinner party this evening and I too am a woman short.'

Oh God, that's the last thing I need, was all Kristin could think. To be forced to sit at the same table as Grant Hunter, knowing she dare not divulge her and her fellow protesters' plans. She mustn't give Grant any warning of what they were about to do. He'd block the entrance to the field for sure.

'Well, I don't . . . ' she began.

But Eve wasn't to be denied. 'Of course you'll attend, darling. Maureen and George are coming with their son and his fiancée. You remember Craig?' She paused, looking slightly nervous it had to be said. Within seconds, Kristin knew the reason for that. 'Plus Daniel, Grant's son. He too has just recently arrived. He's staying with Grant for a day or two while he moves into an apartment on the other side of the village. He's bought the entire ground floor of Woodcote Hall, no less.'

She gave a nervous giggle. Kristin stared at her. Her mother never giggled, nervously or not. Whatever had come over her? Huh! As if she didn't know.

Grant Hunter, that's what. Maybe he liked his women to act as if they were sixteen again? Another reason to hate him. He was consigning her mother to a second girlhood. 'I've not met him before,' Eve was now saying, 'but I'm sure you two will get on.' However, the expression on her face as she said the words belied that outward display of confidence.

★   ★   ★

Once Grant had gone, Eve regarded her daughter with narrow-eyed suspicion and asked, 'Okay, now — what are your real plans? I presume you're not here just to visit me?'

'Well, not entirely, no,' Kristin muttered

Eve cast her eyes upwards in hopeless despair. 'Oh, don't tell me. You're planning some sort of campaign over the meadow.'

'We-ell, yes — '

'Just you? Or have your . . . *friends* — '

She witheringly emphasized the word. ' — come too?'

'Some of them are coming tomorrow and yes, we are going to set up a protest site.'

'For heaven's sake, Kristin, it's too late. It's a done deal. Local people are all for it. It will bring jobs, money, which we're sorely in need of. What shops we've got are in danger of closing.'

'Mum,' Kristin cried, 'they're planning to build over ancient artefacts!'

'There are no ancient artefacts,' Eve scornfully said. 'nothing of any significance, anyway. It was one man with a metal detector who found a couple of bowls or something. It's a meadow which has served no useful purpose for several years now. It's been allowed to deteriorate. The farmer who owned it, Bill Brookes, is broke. He's getting out of farming. There's no money in it anymore, unless you're one of the big boys with vast tracts of land.'

'Well, maybe someone else could be

allowed to buy it as a working farm and try to make it profitable.'

'Bill tried that, but nobody wanted it. His cattle had to be destroyed; they had bovine TB. It finished him. In any case, the land's not suitable for anything else. He couldn't afford to turn down Grant's offer; a very generous offer, I might add.'

'So what's happening to the actual farm?'

Eve shrugged. 'Grant has bought the whole thing but he has no plans to run it as a farm. He's thinking of converting the house into apartments — or he might renovate it and sell it as just a single house. He's thinking of building several smaller starter homes around it in what was the yard and cowsheds.'

Slightly mollified by this, Kristin contented herself with muttering, 'Well, that apart, we're still going to try and save the meadow. It could become a heritage site.'

Thoroughly exasperated by this time

with her daughter's display of obduracy, she flung her hands upwards and walked out of the room. 'I'll get us some lunch. You can make up your bed while I do it.'

★   ★   ★

That evening Kristin stood in front of her wardrobe, looking at the clothes she'd left behind upon joining the protesters, and wondering what to wear for the wretched dinner party. She pulled out one garment after another, but nothing looked right. So it wasn't surprising that she very quickly had a towering pile of discarded outfits on the bed. She'd never been one for formality even before she'd left home. She'd more often than not opted for trousers — jeans, mostly — and tops. And as for dinner parties . . . Well, it was difficult to hold one in a tent. She grinned at the notion of candlelight dining on a fold-away table and chairs. She could just hear Zen, one of the leading lights of their small group. 'Well posh, eh? Who do you think you are, royalty?'

Eventually, she settled on a pair of navy-blue trousers and a silky cream top that she found tucked away in a drawer. She must have had them for at least five years. She held them up in front of her. Were they a bit dated? Oh, for heaven's sake, did it matter? Mind you, there were a few creases. Still, they would most likely drop out. She certainly didn't want Grant Hunter, or his son, to think she was in any way trying to impress them. So, any creases would simply bear out that desire.

She took a deep breath and struggled to fasten the button on the trousers; she must have put on some weight since the last time she'd worn them. The top was also considerably tighter than she liked; positively figure-hugging, in fact. She considered her reflection in the full-length mirror. It would have to do; she hadn't got the time to change again. Even so, she eyed the extravagant amount of flesh exposed by the V-neck.

It reached lower than she remembered. Was it too much, maybe? She'd always been generously endowed in the bust department. Too generously, in her opinion. She had Eve to thank for that.

She searched through a drawer and found a scarf, then draped it decoratively, thus hiding much of the revealed cleavage. There! Problem solved. The only thing was, she now looked like some sort of demure Victorian maiden — which she most certainly wasn't. No demure Victorian maiden would even consider doing what she intended, let alone have the determination to carry it through.

By the time she returned downstairs, her mother had the dining room table laid with a cream damask tablecloth, and her very best china and glassware. She'd even dragged out some of her own mother's silver cutlery. Kristin had forgotten she even had it. God knew where it had been stored away. She couldn't recall seeing it anywhere. In fact, if she'd thought of it at all, she would have assumed Eve had long ago got rid of it. 'All that cleaning,' she remembered her mother moaning after using it the last time — which must have been what, seventeen, eighteen years ago? It must be; she'd been a child at the time. Eve must really want to impress the Grant men.

A large, shallow bowl of flowers made a scented and highly decorative centrepiece, flanked by candles already lit even though it was still light. From the amount of clanking going on in the kitchen, Eve was deep in the throes of cooking.

'Can I help?' Kristin asked, strolling into the kitchen.

'No, I'm practically done. The guests will be arriving at any minute.' There was the faintest tinge of panic in her tone now. 'You will be polite, won't you?'

'Of course.' Kristin raised her eyebrows as if to imply that to be impolite wasn't her way, but then completely spoilt it by adding, 'As long as Mr

Hunter is polite to me.' When her mother's expression instantly hardened, she quickly asked, 'What's his son like? You must have some idea. Grant must have spoken about him.'

'Well, not really; not much, anyway. He's thirty-one, thirty-two; takes after his father by all accounts. A very smart, astute businessman. Made bucket-loads of money.' She gave a snort of laughter. 'If he can afford to buy the entire ground floor of Woodcote Hall, he must have. I heard it was on the market for one and a half million.'

'And is he in the same sort of business? Destroying our heritage for his own profit?'

'Kristin, please.' Eve was sounding exasperated yet again. 'Don't start. He is in partnership with Grant, yes.'

'Ah-ha, so a heartless vandal, just like his father.'

The doorbell rang at that point, cutting off whatever remark Eve might have been driven to make. Instead, she sent Kristin a look of mute pleading.

'Okay, okay.' Kristin held up a hand in surrender. 'I'll behave for now, and as long as they don't provoke me,' she concluded in a murmur low enough for her mother not to hear.

Eve removed her apron to reveal an elegant navy and white dress, with a neckline even more plunging than Kristin's had been before she'd covered it up. Disregarding her daughter's stare of astonishment, she hastened out into the hallway and Kristin heard her saying, 'Grant, how lovely. You're early.'

'Not too early, I hope?' Grant's deep tones asked.

'No, no. Um — Daniel not with you then?'

'He'll be along in half an hour or so. Had to see someone first; a bit of business, I believe.'

'Okay. Well, come in and have a drink. Kristin,' she said, as she led the way into the sitting room, 'can you get Grant a drink? I need to see to one last thing in the kitchen. I won't be long.' And she hurriedly left the room.

Kristin glared after her. The last thing she'd envisaged, or wanted, was a cosy one-on-one with Grant Hunter. She dreaded to think what her father's thoughts about all this would be — although he'd want Eve to be happy, she was sure of that. He'd died six years ago, felled, completely out of the blue, by a massive heart attack. For a while Kristin had believed her mother would never recover from the shock of it, but, of course, she had — eventually. Thus proving the indomitable resilience of the human spirit.

Dennis Lacey had been a relatively wealthy man, having built up a successful engineering business from scratch, so he'd been able to leave a respectable legacy behind him, most of which had gone to Eve, naturally. However, he had bequeathed a sizeable sum of money to Kristin, enough to allow her to take a sabbatical from her rather boring job in a solicitor's office and, for a while at least, pursue her increasingly passionate desire to try and preserve as much as she could of the countryside for future generations. She'd been doing that for the past nine months now and, along with her equally environmentally conscious friends, had managed to save a valuable woodland, home to an endangered butterfly, as well as another meadow in which rare orchids flourished.

However, the portion of her money that she'd set aside for living expenses wouldn't last for much longer, at most a couple of months — enough time, she hoped, to be able to stop the Grants — and then she needed to put her environmental concerns to one side and find a job once more.

'Kristin.' Grant held out a hand, a broad grin adorning his good-looking face. 'Nice to see you again. Although I have to say, I almost didn't recognise you.'

She ignored what she took to be a gibe about her earlier disreputable appearance and asked, 'What can I get you?' However, mindful of her mother's strictures, she took his hand, though it wasn't much more than a brushing of fingers. She didn't want to be accused later by Eve of bad manners, should Grant decide to mention Kristin's coolness. A tactic she wouldn't put past him. And, sure enough, he registered the slight with a tightening of his mouth and a perceptible hardening of his jaw. She turned to the drinks cabinet.

'A gin and tonic, please,' he said.

Silence descended then between them while Kristin poured his gin and a vodka and tonic for herself. She didn't make a habit of drinking spirits of any sort, but it would undoubtedly help her get through what was promising to be a fraught evening. Father and son to contend with? One would be too much; two would most definitely be overkill. Her heart gave a lurch. Maybe she could plead tiredness and escape to bed. She had driven quite a long way.

She'd just taken her first mouthful when the doorbell rang for the second time. 'I'll get it,' she called to her mother.

This time it was George and Maureen with a young man who couldn't be mistaken for anyone other than their son, Craig. He had developed into a younger version of George, portly and with a substantial moustache; the plump girl at his side must be his fiancée, judging by the flashy ring on her left hand.

'Hello,' George said, not bothering to hide his surprise. 'Didn't know you were home.'

'Only briefly.'

'Oh, Lord, don't tell me — you're here because of the new housing development.'

'I've come to see my mother,' she replied, conscious of Grant Hunter in the next room, who must be able to hear every word. And it wasn't strictly a lie. She had come to see Eve — as well as set up the protest camp.

'Good, good. Well, you know Craig, and this lovely young thing is Felicity, his fiancée. We're very pleased to welcome her to our humble little family.'

Kristin smiled. 'Yes, I had already guessed who she must be.' Had George always sounded this pompous?

'Come in, we're in the sitting room. I'm barman, so . . . ' She led the way in and said, 'I'm sure you know Mr Hunter.'

'Yes, of course. How are you? It's good to see you again.'

It was at this point, and much to Kristin's relief, that Eve reappeared. 'Hello, everyone. Darling, I'll have a red wine, please.'

Yet again, the doorbell buzzed. Kristin busied herself pouring her mother's drink. She'd presumed the 'darling' applied to her and not Grant. Kristin heard her mother cry, 'Ah, you must be Daniel. I'm Eve. Come in, come in. I'll introduce you to everyone. They're all here.'

There was a low murmur of a man's voice, and then Eve was walking back into the room, followed by one of the two men whom Kristin had so furiously berated in the field earlier.

The one who'd prevented her from falling, in fact.

3

Kristin stared, the blood draining from her face and rushing with dizzying speed all the way to her feet. Or that was the way it felt, at any rate.

Oh God! This couldn't be happening.

To be forced to sit at the dinner table with him, after the way she'd spoken to him only that afternoon . . . Desperately, she tried to recall exactly what she'd said. Something about money-grubbers only out for profit. She closed her eyes, hoping that when she opened them again, he would have vanished.

No such luck.

He was still there when she squinted from beneath lowered lids, his face showing no expression at all. Oh, glory be, he hadn't recognised her. After all, dressed as she was at the moment, she looked quite different from how she'd looked earlier. Certainly his father had thought so.

But her hopes that he wouldn't realise who she was were swiftly extinguished when he began to move purposefully towards her, his eyes taking on the gleam that she remembered from their earlier encounter.

'I must say, you scrub up extremely well. I almost didn't recognise you,' he murmured. And just as it had before, his gaze travelled leisurely over her. 'It's nice to see you again. I didn't realise you were Eve's daughter. But then,' he added, grinning sardonically, 'why would I? You didn't tell me your name. Eve's spoken about you to my father.'

'Not in too much detail, I hope.' Furious with him for his opening comment, 'You scrub up extremely well', her retort was a tight-lipped one. Flippin' cheek! However, all she could think was, would Eve have told Grant about her campaigning activities? She hoped not. Forewarned was forearmed, as they said, and she didn't want either of the Hunters doing anything to prevent the group's entry to the field the next morning. Thank heavens they would be arriving early. She'd text Zen as soon as she could to tell him to pull out all the stops and get there as early as humanly possible. Before light, ideally.

'Well, I'm sure she's been discreet.' He tilted his head to one side. 'Tell me; I'm curious. Do you make a habit of berating complete strangers on a regular basis? Or is it just me?' His mouth twitched at the corners.

'No, it's not just you,' she riposted. He wasn't taking her at all seriously. Well, he very soon would. She'd see to that. 'It's anyone who's intent on the destruction of our countryside.'

'Kristin,' Eve pleaded, 'please . . . '

Kristin glanced around the room. Everyone was beginning to look a tad uncomfortable — except for Grant, who, like his son, was making no attempt to hide his amusement. Had Daniel told him what had happened? If he had, he evidently wasn't taking her seriously. Probably had her down as some hysterical, over-emotional female. Well, they'd pretty soon discover she wasn't to be so easily discounted. Her pulses quickened at the thought of the battle that almost certainly lay ahead. These two weren't going to give in easily. They had the look — and self-assurance — of men accustomed to getting their own way in all things.

'I think you might have met your match there, my boy,' Grant laughed.

Daniel's expression was one of calculation now. 'So, are you planning to try and stop the development? I imagine that's what your . . . tirade was all about earlier.'

There was more than a hint of steel now within the silvery eyes. The planes of his face had hardened too, although that couldn't disguise the high, pronounced cheekbones, the long, straight nose, and the mouth, with its almost sensual lower lip. The chiselled jaw line, however, was more than a match for the steely eye. It also hinted at a resolute and unyielding personality. Topping all of this was a thick head of hair the exact colour of dark treacle toffee. All in all, a man to be reckoned with, she nervously decided. And that opinion hadn't taken into account his height — six foot one or two, she estimated — and his powerful, athletic build.

Her heart gave a little jump. She mustn't give anything away. Just as she mustn't make the mistake of underestimating him, or Grant. They hadn't got where they were today by being soft and compassionate. They would have had to be completely unscrupulous; ruthless, even. And there was a certain look to Daniel now — a look that warned her to beware.

She shrugged. 'What can one woman do alone?' She wasn't actually lying; it was just a tactical omission of the fact that her co-campaigners would be joining her tomorrow.

'We-ell, you put up a pretty good fight earlier today, alone. It was impressively feisty, actually.' He cocked his head to one side as he awaited her response to that.

That had almost sounded like a compliment. He couldn't have meant it that way, surely? Although there was a strange little glint in his eye — admiration?

Kristin took a large gulp of her drink. And promptly swallowed it too quickly. Straight away she felt the beginnings of an embarrassing, choking cough. She gasped, and somehow managed to suppress the spasm — although she had a strong suspicion that her face had turned bright red with the effort — and then, just to make matters worse, she felt the sting of tears in her eye.

For all that, though, she managed to ignore the hint of mirth on Daniel's face again, despite the almost overwhelming urge to swipe it away. He knew only too well what had happened. Yet again, a flash of hatred for him consumed her. He'd probably have taken some sort of sadistic pleasure in seeing her choke and collapse in front of him.

But all he said was a low, 'Okay?'

'Come along, everyone.' Eve hastened to intervene; she was clearly afraid things were going to escalate into a full-blown row. 'Dinner is ready. If you all go through to the dining room, Kristin and I will serve up. Come, Kristin.'

* * *

Talk, not unexpectedly, proved a little stilted to begin with; but once the wine began to flow, tongues started to loosen.

'So, Kristin,' George began, having plumped himself down by the side of her. Grant, unfortunately had chosen to sit on her other side, although she supposed that was a great deal better than having Daniel there. 'Tell me what you've been doing with yourself?'

'Oh, you know, moving around a bit. It makes life more interesting.'

'Your mum said you were on one of these protest things,' Maureen interjected. 'You know, like Greenham Common all those years ago.'

Kristin saw Daniel's head jerk as he stared her way. He'd heard Maureen's words. Damn! He'd realise now that she was an active protester and, from the look of him, he'd pretty soon work out what that would mean for his and his father's plans. Because from what she'd seen and heard about him so far, he was miles away from being stupid. She gnawed at her bottom lip. She'd have to say something to remove any suspicion he might have about her motives for being here.

'Well . . . ' Kristin eyed him and then her mother, who was giving her the evil eye in a clear warning to remember her promise. She'd obviously also overheard her friend's remark. 'I didn't do much really. It was more like a holiday camp. You know, camp fires, lots of singing.'

She heard Daniel give a snort

— whether of amusement or derision she'd have been hard pressed to say. Fortunately, he'd chosen to sit on the opposite side of the table, up a bit from her. So it was a simple matter to ignore him.

However, he clearly had other ideas. 'That's not what a friend of mine said,' he commented. 'He told me a group of protesters created havoc on some site near to him. They did more damage to the environment than anything that the developers had planned. Bolts in trees, platforms in branches, tunnels dug everywhere, barricades erected, natural flora trampled and all but destroyed, piles of rubbish everywhere, clothes lines . . . How on earth can you call that protecting the countryside?' He snorted a second time. There was no mistake now; it signified derision, contempt, even. Any suggestion of admiration had vanished.

As a result, Kristin's tone hardened, as did her eyes. Even so, she didn't as much as glance his way. She continued to address herself solely to George. 'Sometimes these things are necessary. One has to take the long view. A little damage — '

'A little damage?' Daniel exclaimed. 'Gavin's description made it sound like a bomb site.'

'A little damage,' she repeated, more forcefully now, but still not looking his way, 'can prevent wholesale destruction, which surely must be the right way to go?'

'Well, don't get any ideas about doing anything like that here,' he went on. 'Because we'll have you removed before you can say heave ho.'

Kristin swept her gaze to him then. Heave ho? What did he think this was, some sort of tug-of-war? Which, she belatedly supposed, it was — in a way.

'Um, has everyone finished their beef?' Eve hastily said, leaping to her feet and starting to remove the empty plates. 'Kristin, I need your help in the kitchen.'

Kristin dutifully picked up the

remaining plates and followed her mother out of the room. Eve didn't quite slam the plates down onto the worktop. Even so, they made a dangerous clatter.

'What do you think you are doing?' She rounded on Kristin, her eyes blazing, her cheeks a deep crimson.

'What I'm doing?' Kristin echoed indignantly. She felt her mother's anger with her was a little unfair. She'd remained perfectly polite throughout the . . . discussion, for want of a better description. It had been Daniel who'd been rude and argumentative. 'I'm not doing anything. I didn't bring the subject up, Maureen did.'

'That's not the point,' Eve hissed. Clearly, she was keen not to be overheard in the dining room.

'Then what is?'

'I forbid you to start anything here in the village. I have my name and-and my reputation to consider. What will people think? That I have some sort of hippy daughter?'

Kristin couldn't help it; she burst out laughing. 'Hippy? I'm not a hippy. They went out with the seventies.'

'Just keep off the subject of the wretched field — environment, whatever. I mean it, Kristin. I'm not having my dinner party ruined.'

They returned to the dining room with the dessert, a delicious-looking summer fruit pudding, accompanied by an enormous bowl of clotted cream. Being in love must have gone to Eve's head, Kristin decided then, because previously she wouldn't have allowed clotted cream through the front door, never mind on her dinner table.

Grant took one look at Eve's flushed face and said, 'That looks absolutely gorgeous, love. You sit down. I'm sure Kristin won't mind serving it up.' It wasn't a suggestion; it was a direct order.

Kristin tightened her lips in vexation at his authoritarian manner, but not wanting to embark upon another . . . discussion, this time with the father rather than the son, she did as he'd said. She'd already decided that Grant Hunter was going to be a pretty formidable opponent. One she'd need to tread warily with, she suspected. Who knew what he'd be capable of — he and his son — in the face of some serious opposition to his money-making agenda?

Once again, she ignored the glitter within Daniel's gaze. A frisson of unease did ripple through her, though. Thank goodness Zen and the gang would be here in the morning. She was definitely going to require their backup — as feisty as Daniel considered her. She just hoped they'd be in time and Daniel wouldn't have already blocked the entrance to the field.

She allowed herself a slanting glance at him as she handed him his dish of pudding, only to encounter a look that was still glittering — but with renewed amusement rather than contempt. He was openly relishing her being forced to kowtow to his father and he wasn't bothering to hide it. She was sorely tempted, there and then, to throw his pudding at him; only good manners — and her mother's predictable fury with her — prevented her from doing so. Instead she contented herself with dark thoughts of all the terrible things she'd like to do to him. They were hateful, both him and his father. Wreckers, the pair of them. How could her mother have allowed herself to get involved with them?

The talk after that turned to more commonplace matters — to Eve's palpable relief. Even Daniel seemed to have decided to let matters rest, because he turned to Craig and Felicity and began to quiz them about their wedding plans.

Kristin sat in silence, allowing the conversation to flow around her. That was until Grant leant in to her and quietly said, 'Your mother worries about you, you know.'

'Well, she needn't. I'm a big girl now. I can make my own decisions, do what I want, look after myself, even,' she ended with a generous dollop of sarcasm. Who did he think he was, telling her what her mother thought or felt?

Undaunted, Grant went on, 'Yes, but see things from her viewpoint. You're her daughter, her only daughter; and, by the sound of it, you're off fraternising with God knows who and doing God knows what.'

She didn't have to listen to this, from him of all people. The man who was hell-bent on despoiling their village. Abruptly she got to her feet. 'Would anyone like coffee?' She could see that Grant had got her meaning.

A resigned expression came over his face as he said, 'Well, I would, and then I must get off. Early start in the morning.'

And Kristin simply couldn't stop herself. 'Oh, why's that? To begin your destruction of the meadow before anyone's out of bed?'

Conversation halted completely and

everyone stared at her. Her mother was transfixed with horror. Kristin gnawed at her bottom lip. Oh Lord, now she'd done it. She waited for the storm to break around her.

But it was her mother who spoke first. 'Kristin!' she cried. 'You apologise — right now.'

Grant held up a hand to her. 'It's okay, Eve. She has a right to ask.' He looked back at Kristin then. 'We're not planning anything immediately. We don't want to rush.'

'Oh, really,' she said.

'Yes, really,' was his low answer. 'We're keen to give people time to adjust to the idea of what's going to happen.'

'And if they don't adjust, what then? You'll bulldoze anyway?'

Grant stared straight at her, his gaze as steely as his son's had been earlier.

A stab of misgiving pierced Kristin.

'Don't get any silly ideas about setting up any sort of protest camp in the field, because, as Daniel has already said, it won't work.'

She didn't answer. Instead, she glanced around at her mother and the other guests and said, 'If you'll all excuse me, I'm tired. It's been a long day, so I think I'll go — '

Daniel cut in at that, his words blunt and straight to the point. 'To bed or to the field?'

Again, Kristin didn't respond. Not that Daniel gave her the time.

'Because if that's the plan,' he went on, 'you'll very quickly discover that you've taken on more than you bargained for. Considerably more.'

4

The second that Kristin reached her bedroom she pulled out her mobile phone, at the same time muttering to herself, 'It's not me who's going to have more than I bargained for, Daniel Grant. Within a very short time, you're going to be wondering what's hit you. Yes, indeed.'

She began to text Zen but then decided to speak to him instead. A text just wouldn't do at the moment. She needed to vent her wrath and she knew Zen would let her.

'Hi, Kristin,' his response was instantaneous. 'I was just about to call you. We've arrived, made good time.'

'You're here, in Bentleigh?' she cried, unable to believe the news. 'That's wonderful.' And it was. The Grants hadn't had the opportunity to do anything to prevent their entry to the field. Perfect.

'Yeah. Your directions were spot-on. We're just going in. There's not even a lock on the gate. Not that that would stop us, but, even so — ' He chuckled. ' — it means we won't need to mess around with cutters.'

'I'll be there as early as I can in the morning. We've got a real fight on our hands, I can tell you. We can't let them win this; we simply can't.'

And if her present resolve was due, in part, to fury with the sheer arrogance of the two Grant men rather than her fervent desire to protect any retrievable archaeological treasures that might be found, then she disregarded it.

* * *

The following morning Kristin was up early; dawn had already broken over the horizon, and the sun was steadily rising, casting a golden glow over everything. The birds were in full singing mode, blissfully heralding the start of what promised to be yet another hot day. The country had been in the grip of a heat wave for some time now and the temperature, even at this time, felt as if it were in the high teens.

She quietly let herself out of the house and climbed into her car. She'd written a short note to her mother, explaining where she'd gone and saying that she'd be back later. She hoped Eve wouldn't be too angry with her and would try to understand that she had to do this. She still hadn't told her mother that this would be her last protest, because, frankly, she didn't have the foggiest idea how long it would last. These things could go on for months; years even. Not that she would last that long. As she'd already decided, she'd soon need to start her search for a job. She knew she wouldn't find one here in Bentleigh. She'd have to look further afield, for sure. She fancied Birmingham. The trouble was it was too far to commute, which was why she was retaining enough of her inheritance to put down a sizable deposit on an apartment — not in Birmingham, that would be too expensive — but hopefully somewhere on the outskirts.

She drove through the village and then along the lane that led to the meadow. There was no one about yet, so there was no one to see her or hear the sound of her vehicle passing through, for the engine was becoming increasingly noisy. There were also a number of scratches and dents on its bodywork. As soon as she had a job, she'd consider exchanging it for a newer model. Till then, it would have to do.

When she finally reached the gateway into the meadow, she couldn't believe her eyes. There was already a small encampment of tents, and platforms were in the process of being constructed in a couple of trees. When finished they would have tarpaulins for shelter, and rope ladders for climbing, which could be swiftly pulled up when necessary to prevent access by the developers bent on removing the protesters from the branches. The remaining trees, and there were another two, would have wire wrapped around their trunks, to prevent the use of chainsaws. They would also erect a simple hut to hold their food supplies and other stores and keep it all dry. There was even a fire going, upon which a couple of the women were cooking what smelt like breakfast. Her stomach rumbled noisily. She hadn't lingered to eat, not wanting anything to delay her return to the meadow.

Zen was standing inside the gateway, clearly having heard the sounds of her imminent arrival. It was a miracle that Eve hadn't heard her leaving the driveway of the house. She normally had hearing that, Kristin was positive, could detect a feather landing on a cushion half a mile away. She'd have tried to persuade her to abandon the protest, for sure.

Kristin parked and swiftly climbed out. Zen strode over to her and swept her into his arms. 'Hello, love.' He then bent his head and kissed her warmly; enthusiastically, even. For the first time, Kristin didn't welcome it. She pulled away.

'What's up?' His chocolate-brown eyes narrowed beneath the heavy fringe of dark blond hair as he scrutinised her. His normally good-humoured expression was one of deliberately exaggerated hurt. 'Haven't you missed me then?'

She couldn't help grinning at his play-acting. 'It's only been a day.'

'I know, but I don't operate fully without you,' he mendaciously said. Zen had never needed anyone, as far as she knew. He was a totally independent, free spirit. He eyed her. 'You look worried.' For all their casual relationship, he knew her better than anyone. Must be the result of spending the last nine months in each other's company.

'Well, that's because I am.'

'Let me guess — Hunter?'

'Yes, him. It's all been a bit . . . well, awkward.'

He arched an expectant eyebrow.

'There's two of them, father and son. I met them last night. My mother's — um, involved with Hunter senior.'

'Is she? Very involved?' The eyebrow went even higher.

'Uh-huh.'

'That's going to make life difficult. For you, anyway.'

Kristin nodded. 'Precisely. They came to dinner last evening; but before that, on my way home, I saw Daniel. I didn't know it was him, of course. He was here, with another man; they were obviously studying what looked like a large plan of the development. I couldn't help myself; I stopped and told them what I thought of them.'

'Did you, now?' His expression was one of admiration. 'Good for you. So have they sussed what we're about to do?'

'They've a pretty good idea. One of the other dinner guests let it drop that I've been at a couple of other protest camps. Daniel picked that up straight away and warned me off; told me that any sort of protest would be futile. They'll just remove us.'

'Huh! Let them try. Bring it on, guys, I say.' He slanted a glance at her. 'Do they realise you won't be alone?'

'I don't think so.' She wasn't at all sure about that, though. Daniel had certainly looked suspicious.

'Good girl. Mustn't give too much away. So — ' Zen was suddenly business-like once more. ' — we need to start on a trench . . . '

'Where?'

'Inside the gateway and beyond. Deep and wide enough to ensure they can't get us out quickly or easily. Or, more to the point, get in.'

'You'll be careful, though, won't you? We don't want to damage anything that might be buried.'

'Course I will. Don't worry. You go and get some breakfast. I don't suppose you've had any.' There were sounds of people approaching from behind them. They both turned to see Shrimp — real name Stanley, but they always called him Shrimp because of his lack of inches — striding over, along with other members of their group.

'Hey,' he said, 'how are ya?'

'I'm good,' Kristin said. 'And you?'

'Fine, yeah, fine.' He hugged her warmly, as did a couple of other young men. 'It's real nice to see ya again.'

'I've only been gone for a day,' she once more pointed out.

'I know, but we missed you.'

She had, more than once, suspected that Shrimp was growing a little too fond of her. She slanted a glance at Zen; he grinned knowingly. Clearly, he saw the same thing. He didn't look at all worried — or jealous, despite the fact that he and she had enjoyed a casual, very on and off relationship for the past months. Nothing heavy: the odd cuddle, a kiss. It suited her — and she suspected it suited Zen. She, for one, didn't want any sort of romantic involvement, not at this stage of her life, and certainly not in the event of her plans to leave them. Although she hadn't said anything about that to Zen.

'Okay, fellas,' he called, 'let's get digging.'

★ ★ ★

Within a very short space of time, they had a wide trench dug along the entire width of the gateway and beyond. As Zen had said, it would very effectively prevent any sort of unwanted entry other than that of a tank, and she really didn't envisage the Hunters having one of those at their disposal. Although having met them, nothing would surprise her. The protesters themselves would lay planks of wood across it as and when they needed to get out.

Meanwhile, the women had been fixing banners onto the lane side of the hedgerows, all proclaiming, HANDS OFF THIS FIELD. STOP YOUR DESTRUCTION OF OUR LAND. THIS IS AN ANCIENT BATTLE-FIELD. Each one had been written in bright red paint on a white background.

Kristin couldn't believe that so much had been accomplished in such a short time. It was nothing short of a miracle. Just wait till Daniel and his father saw this. It should stop them in their tracks.

'Let's start wrapping the wire round the other trees now and sink poles into the ground just behind the hedgerow — suspend wire between them, in case they decide to force entry through the hedge.' It would make for a good barrier — unless they brought wire cutters, of course. Kristin smiled grimly. It would nevertheless slow them down and allow the campaigners to form a human barrier of sorts.

By mid-day they'd done all they could. It would be a waiting game now until the Hunters decided to show up. Cars had been driving along the lane all morning while they worked, honking horns, arms pushed out of windows to wave, whether in a show of support or anger wasn't clear. One man did shout, 'What the hell do you think you're doing? No one wants you here. Clear off. Load of parasites . . . '

But by late afternoon there was still no sign of either of the Hunter men. Yet they must be aware of the arrival of the protesters by now? Maybe they were hoping local opinion would do the job of driving the campaigners away for them and so save them the trouble? Well, if that was their game, they were set to be disappointed. A few passing jeers and insults wouldn't deter them. These were people who were more than accustomed to such tactics. In fact, it only served to harden their determination to stay put.

When three days had passed, however, with absolutely no sign of either Daniel or Grant, Kristin became aware of a vague sense of — what? Disappointment? Frustration? Disquiet? She was keen to get their first confrontation over with. Demonstrate to both men that they had a real battle on their hands.

She'd returned to her mother's house each evening and spent the night. But

Eve's air of disapproval was growing increasingly oppressive; so much so that on the fourth night she said, 'Look, Mum, you obviously don't want me here.'

'That's not true. I just don't want what you're doing. It's so . . . well, embarrassing for me. People are blaming me for your actions. Sara Crosby actually crossed the road to avoid me yesterday afternoon. She always stops for a chat — It's horrible; humiliating. I'm losing friends.'

'I'm sorry; I really am.'

'Then stop it — please. People don't want you here. Any of you. I drove past the camp yesterday- and I have to say, some of them don't even look clean.' She gave an exaggerated shudder. 'I don't know how you can mix with them. You could catch something. We brought you up to be better than this. To do something with your life.'

'Mum, I am doing something with my life; something worthwhile. Surely you can see that? The protesters — well, they're nice people; you should come and meet them. They're simply concerned for our heritage — as I am.'

'No, you're spitefully stopping progress. If you all had your way, we'd still be living in mud huts, and cooking on open fires. Oh, but then you are, aren't you?' she scoffed.

'Have you talked to Grant?' Kristin diplomatically interrupted this tirade.

'Of course.'

'I presume he knows what we've done here in the meadow?'

'Yes, he does.'

Kristin was puzzled. 'So . . . ' She frowned at her mother. 'Why hasn't he been along to the meadow? I mean he was quite adamant — they both were, him and his beastly son — that they'd remove us. By force was the implication.'

'Grant isn't the sort of man who goes looking for trouble.'

Kristin gave a loud snort. 'Huh! I bet his son is, though.'

Eve disregarded that. 'He's hoping it will fizzle out of its own accord. That you'll realise the local community is solidly behind him and so give up.'

'He'll wait a very long time if that's the only plan he has — ' She eyed her mother. 'And Daniel — is he playing the same waiting game?'

Eve shrugged. 'As far as I know. He hasn't been here since the other evening. He had some business of his own in London.'

In the end, it seemed easier all round — and fairer to her mother — for Kristin to remain in one of the tents at the camp, rather than shuffle between home and the meadow. So the next morning she decided to leave the car at the house for now and packed a small, easily portable bag with a few essentials, plus some changes of clothes, and walked back to the camp.

She heard the sounds of shouting before she could actually see the field. Her heart lurched. She broke into a jog. What was happening? It must be the Hunters. Were they in the process of carrying out their threats? They'd certainly picked their moment — when she was absent. Had they known that? Surely her mother wouldn't have tipped Grant off? Although she couldn't imagine what difference her presence — or not — would make to them.

She was running fast by the time she reached the gateway, which ensured that she'd picked up enough speed to leap the ditch, bag and all. She landed hard and fell to her knees, dropping her bag as she did so. Despite this, she could see quite clearly what was going on.

There were two people, each on horseback, riding around the edge of the camp, imperiously surveying all that was going on. She had no trouble recognising the man. It was Daniel. But with him was a woman she didn't know; a very poised, self-confident woman if her bearing was anything to go by. She sat straight-backed upon her horse, her head held high, a sneer decorating her lips.

Kristin hated her on sight.

5

Kristin scrambled up from her knees, retrieved her bag, and began to head for the riders. They must have leapt the ditch just as she had. Only in their cases, being on horseback would have made the exercise a whole lot easier. She and Zen couldn't have foreseen that the opposition would arrive mounted rather than in a vehicle of some sort. Daniel must have known about the trench, which meant he must have had someone spying on them.

The protesters were standing closely together, watching the pair riding around them, clearly trying to anticipate what they were going to do next.

Zen shouted, 'Okay, what do you want? Who are you?'

Daniel didn't respond; he carried on around the perimeter of the meadow, for all the world as if he were simply out for a pleasurable ride. His companion was pointing at the tents, her head turned, her expression one of utter contempt.

Kristin was almost level with the two of them before Daniel swivelled his head and saw her. He pulled his horse to a stop immediately and sat, every bit as haughty and proud as his female companion. She asked, 'Daniel, why have you stopped?' Then she saw Kristin. 'Do you know her?' she demanded.

Daniel's expression throughout this remained impenetrable. There was no indication of either the amusement or the contempt he'd exhibited at Eve's. In fact, it was as if he were wearing a mask, through which only his silvery eyes glittered down at her. 'You could say that,' he murmured. 'Hello, Kristin.'

'What do you want?'

'To see what you're up to.' He didn't remove his gaze from her. He sat on his horse, his bearing one of complete self-possession. There could be no mistaking it: he was supremely confident of his right to be there. Which wasn't surprising; his father — and he, presumably — did own the land he and his horse were standing upon, after all. It was Kristin and her fellow campaigners who were the trespassers.

'Well, now that you've seen, you can leave again.'

'Oh, don't worry, I will — eventually.' He stood up in the stirrups, scanning the field surrounding their tents. 'I can see you and your fellow travellers have made their customary mark upon the area — and not for the better.'

'We're not travellers, we're eco-campaigners. There is a difference.'

'Oh my God,' the woman said. 'Some campaigners! You all look like tramps. Why don't you get jobs? I suppose you're all on some sort of benefit?' She sneered. 'At the taxpayers' expense.'

Kristin didn't dignify that remark with an answer. It was no one else's business where the protesters obtained their money to live, and she for one

73

most certainly wasn't living at the taxpayers' expense.

'By the way, Kristin, meet Sophie — a friend.'

Kristin couldn't help but notice Sophie's surprised glance at him. She obviously considered herself more than a mere friend. Kristin realised, now that she was closer to her, exactly how beautiful, poised and elegant Sophie was. Her riding outfit, for example, must have cost a fortune and had probably been tailor-made for her. Which, she supposed, wasn't surprising. She couldn't imagine Daniel with anyone less than perfect. He was, despite his many faults, a very handsome man. She would imagine he could have his pick of women — except for her, of course. She wouldn't touch him with a thirty-foot telegraph pole.

'So,' he drawled, 'what are you planning to do, exactly?'

'What it looks like — defend a valuable piece of land and protect whatever lies beneath the surface until anything that's here can be safely excavated.'

Daniel snorted. 'That didn't stop you digging a damn great trench though, did it? Possibly destroying some of your precious artefacts in the process?'

Kristin had her mouth open to deny having damaged anything, when Sophie said, 'You surely don't think there's actually anything valuable here, do you?' She gave a sneering laugh. 'Okay, a local treasure hunter and his trusty metal detector uncovered a couple of bowls. It's hardly in the same league as the Staffordshire hoard.'

Daniel was still studying Kristin intently. In fact, she didn't think he'd taken his eyes off her since he'd first spotted her. What was his problem? Had she got dirt on her face? Or were her top buttons undone again? A discreet glance down at herself revealed that they weren't — so what was he staring so rudely at? She tilted her head and returned his gaze defiantly. Still, he didn't look away.

'Kristin.' It was Zen. He had moved silently to her side while she and Daniel had continued to fence with their eyes. He slipped an arm around her shoulders. She saw Daniel clock the gesture and watched curiously as his eyes darkened until they were the colour of wet slate. 'Everything okay?'

'Perfectly,' she said. 'This is Daniel Hunter and his . . . friend.' She deliberately emphasized the word and watched as Sophie's eyes also darkened — with annoyance, in her case. What Daniel's emotion had been, she had no idea, 'Sonya, isn't it?'

'No, it's Sophie,' was the snapped reply to that — which, of course, Kristin had known very well. She'd just had a sudden urge to wipe the superior expression from the other woman's face.

'Aah,' breathed Zen, 'I should have guessed. The vandal himself.'

'Oh, for God's sake.' This exclamation of irritation came from Sophie.

'Come on, Daniel, I think we've seen enough.'

Daniel still said nothing, although his gaze had finally left Kristin and had settled upon Zen. 'And you are?' he asked.

'Zen, a . . . friend of Kristin's.'

He was taking the mickey now, Kristin knew. She smothered a chuckle.

'I see.' Daniel slanted his gaze back to Kristin. 'Well, my father and I warned you not to try this.'

'So you did,' she murmured with deliberate provocation. 'And whoop-de-doo, what do you know? I ignored you.'

'You won't stop us, Kristin. We will have you removed. All of this — ' He waved his hand, indicating the defences they'd erected, the trees with their platforms, the tents. ' — will be no more effective than a row of match-sticks. It will all be swept away.'

'Oh, and what happened to your father's intent to give everyone time to adjust?'

His eyes narrowed. 'Don't make the

mistake of underestimating us.'

'And you just try and remove us,' she challenged, 'and see how far you get.'

She watched then, grinning broadly, as he turned his horse and he and Sophie began to ride back towards the gateway.

She gave Zen a high five and snorted, 'First blood to us, I think. Although,' she added in an undertone, 'if they're really determined to get us out, they will — eventually. But we'll put up a damned good fight first.'

'That's my girl,' he laughed. 'And who knows — they might decide it's not worth the hassle and give up. It's happened before, after all.'

'Mmm, I'm not sure it will this time. It strikes me that the Hunters are a pretty formidable team. You haven't met his father yet. Despite his reasonable-sounding words, he's some- one who's extremely accustomed to having his own way about everything. As is his son, I suspect.' And she gazed thoughtfully at the pair riding away from them.

But things took a turn for the better a couple of mornings later when a representative from the local historical society showed up. One of the campaigners directed him towards Kristin and Zen, whereupon he introduced himself as Richard Millard.

'I'm the president of the Huntleigh Historical and Countryside Preservation Society,' he told them.

The title sounded as if it should be set to music, Kristin thought. Maybe something in the pom-pom-pom style of Gilbert and Sullivan? She smothered a wayward giggle.

'How did you hear about this-this planned destruction of a valuable historical site?' he went on to ask, sublimely oblivious to Kristin's hastily suppressed laughter.

'My mother manages to get the local paper to me now and again,' she told him, 'wherever I am, and I read an article about it in that. It mentioned your society, so we thought we'd come along and see if we could help.'

'Good, good. Well, I can see you've made a promising start.' He rubbed his hands together, his smile one of extreme satisfaction. 'We need to join forces. We're very keen to discover what exactly could be buried here. We did try to get the planning permission rescinded, to no avail. Between you and me,' he muttered, leaning in towards Kristin, 'the Hunters have friends in high places; very high, indeed. And we were told to desist in very strong terms.'

'Really?' Kristin exclaimed. Although why she should be surprised, she didn't know. She'd already had her own suspicions regarding corruption in high places. 'Exactly who — as in friends?'

'Well, I can't tell you that.' His expression was an evasive one and Kristin found herself wondering if he was being quite truthful. 'I can tell you that we're very grateful, and thankful, that you've turned up. The more hands to the helm, so to speak, the better.'

'Quite,' agreed Zen. This was just what they needed: strong local support.

'I can see you've made great progress in your defences. May I ask your names?'

'Oh yes — sorry. I'm Kristin Lacey and this is Zen. Well, Saracen Keeble to be exact. We all call him Zen. Less of a mouthful.'

With an expression that had warmed the longer he regarded Kristin, Richard held out his hand to her. 'I hear you've done this before, uh — Kristin. Is it okay if I call you that?'

'Well, it is my name.' She grinned at him.

'I didn't wish to seem presumptuous.' He coughed gently behind a raised hand.

Kristin really did have to fight to conceal her mirth then. She'd put him at around thirty — going on sixty. But hey, his support would be a bonus, especially if his society had a number of members who would also offer their help. 'So, how many of you, are there? The more the merrier, as they say, and we need all the local support we can get.'

He cleared his throat and said, 'At the present time we only number seven, I'm afraid.'

'S-seven?' Kristin stammered. Why on earth did a society of just seven members need a president?

'Yes, and they're all ... well, somewhat elderly.'

Kristin took that to mean too old to camp out in a field. So no help to be had there, then.

'However, we're very optimistic that more will join us once word gets around,' he went on. 'We're a relatively new society, but becoming involved in your fight should hopefully garner us a good deal of publicity and thereby extra members. I've contacted the local newspapers again. One has agreed to send someone along to do a more in-depth interview with you all, now that you're here.' He swivelled his head at the sound of a vehicle in the lane. 'In fact, that could well be him now.'

And indeed it was. Two men climbed from the vehicle that parked in the gateway, only to stand looking down into the trench. They were both loaded down with bags and a camera, so they wouldn't be able to leap the gap — as clearly Richard Millard had done.

'Hang on,' Zen called, 'I'm coming.'

He strode across to them, picking up a couple of planks as he went. Within minutes the two men had negotiated the makeshift bridge and were on their way towards Kristin and Richard.

Richard moved to greet them. 'Thank you for coming. I'm Richard Millard, president of the historical society. It was me who contacted you. This is Kristin Lacey, who is spearheading the campaign against the proposed development.'

'Hi,' said the two men in unison. 'We're from the *Gazette*. So who's going to give us the lowdown on progress so far?'

'Well . . . ' Richard allowed himself a modest smile. 'Kristin, would you care to?'

'Sure, why not?'

The interviewer pulled a small tape recorder from his bag and held it in front of her. 'I believe you're originally from the village. Tell me, what did you do before becoming involved with this campaign?'

'Oh — um, I joined the protesters about nine months ago on another campaign, but before that I worked for a local solicitor.'

'What made you give up your job for — well, this?' He indicated the campsite.

'I wanted to protect the countryside from any more environmental damage. So when I learnt that this housing development was in the offing in my home village on what could turn out to be a valuable battle site, I managed to persuade some of my co-campaigners to come here and fight.'

'Isn't it a bit extreme, not to say rash,

abandoning a perfectly good job?'

'I didn't think so. At the time, I was planning a change in my lifestyle anyway.'

'But such a huge change?'

'Yes, but to return to the point of this interview. As you already know,' she went on, 'the development here is going to consist of homes priced at one million pounds plus, thus reaping rich, not to say, extortionate, profits for the Hunter Association. As your previous article pointed out, and, as I wish to emphasize, this will be to the great detriment of the local environment and its infrastructure, as well as the destruction of an unknown quantity of what could be very ancient artefacts, possibly dating back as far as the fifteenth century and the Wars of the Roses. We aim to do all that we can to prevent this.'

'With the help of the Historic and Countryside Preservation Society, naturally,' Richard chipped in.

'I see.' The reporter seemed to

dismiss Richard as someone of no significance at all and swept his gaze back to Kristin. 'Now as you've said, you've done this sort of thing before, Ms Lacey.'

'Call me Kristin, please. If I might just point out, and as I'm sure you can see, it's not only me; there's fifteen of us at the moment, headed by Zen and myself. People come and go, obviously, but we're usually a much larger group. And yes, we have done this before. I've only been present on a couple of the protests. As I have already said, I only joined the campaigners nine months ago. They've usually been successful, however.' At this point she gave a self-deprecating smile. 'Sometimes the opposition is simply too powerful and we have to surrender to the inevitable, but not before causing a great deal of trouble and expense for the developers.'

'But surely, a village like Bentleigh needs fresh blood — residents — to survive?' The interviewer pushed the recorder even closer to her, as if he didn't want to miss a single word in the recording. Either that or he wanted to intimidate her. He had sounded critical of her actions once or twice. 'I mean — there's already talk of closing the local primary school because there aren't enough children to fill it. Wouldn't this development maybe help stop that happening?'

'Well, yes — if the new owners are young enough to have small children. But I would have thought the prospective buyers of one-million-pound-plus houses would be past the age of childbearing. They'd be more mature people, surely?'

'Not necessarily,' he argued. 'And what about the extra customers for the local shops?'

Kristin snorted. 'They'll go to the nearest supermarket for most of their stuff. I mean — I doubt any of the village shops would stock quails eggs or caviar, and that's what those sort of people would demand.'

'Isn't that a bit classist?' the reporter said.

Richard leant in to point out, 'It's not just about the possible future residents of these houses — it's about the possibility of priceless treasures being uncovered, right here where we're standing. Do we really want to risk destroying a possible second valuable hoard? Just to bring fresh people into the village? Isn't our heritage more important, and the preservation of it?'

'Yeah, I see. Well, how about some pics? Of you, love.' He regarded Kristin with visible appreciation. 'You look pretty photogenic to me. It's a sure way of grabbing the reader's attention if you feature a pretty girl. They look at the picture and then read the article, and that's what you want.'

However, Kristin didn't want to be photographed simply because of her looks. But then again, if it reaped good publicity for their cause, how could she say no? 'Okay. But hang on; it mustn't be just me. We're all involved in this, and then there's the camp site. A photograph of that would prove to your readers that we're not damaging the very environment that we're fighting to protect.' She hadn't forgotten Daniel's accusation on the night of her mother's dinner party. That the protesters destroyed the very things that they were supposedly protecting. She was determined to prove him wrong.

Finally, with the photographs duly taken of firstly Kristin alone, and then Kristin, Zen and Shrimp, the two newspapermen left again. Richard didn't seem to want to follow suit, however. 'Now, what can I do to help?' he asked. 'I'll do anything. You only have to say the word.'

'Okay, thanks,' Zen at last spoke. 'All the work's done, but if your members feel like coming along and mucking in, they'd be very welcome. We have some spare tents.'

'Oh, well, I don't know about that,' Richard murmured, thus confirming Kristin's supposition of them being too old to rough it in a field. 'But you can rely on their support in talking about the cause and the wrongs of what is being planned here. And, naturally, I'll be a regular visitor.' His warm gaze moved back to Kristin again. 'You can be sure of that,' he murmured. 'Now, is there anything you need? Food? My mother's a great cook. I'm sure she'd prepare you hot meals and I could transport them here — providing I can get my car into the field.' He glanced back at the gateway, the planks having been once again removed. 'She's very keen to be involved in this campaign.'

'Car's no problem,' Zen assured him. 'The planks make a very good bridge. We've already tried them ourselves. So, yeah — food would be great. There are limitations to what can be cooked over a camp fire.'

*   *   *

Once Richard had left, Zen nudged her and said, along with a wicked smile, 'I think you scored there, my girl. He hardly gave the rest of us a glance.'

'Oh, I wouldn't say that,' Kristin airily replied. 'Anyway, he's not my type. Although I won't be saying no to some of his mum's home cooking. And talking of mums, I think I'll go back and see mine tonight. She'll only get miffed if I leave it too long. Plus I can launder my clothes, charge my phone, and have a bath.' She lifted an arm and sniffed. 'Phew! Yeah, I definitely need a bath.'

As she walked back to the village and her mother's house, she gave a little more thought to what Zen had said about Richard and his rather pointed partiality for her. He had concentrated on her, it was true, to the point of embarrassment once or twice. That was the last thing she needed, a man coming on to her. Maybe she could persuade Zen to make it look as if she and he were an item. Actions could sometimes speak louder than words. And it wouldn't actually be a lie.

She smiled to herself. She liked Zen.

He was attractive, with a pronounced sense of humour that had reduced her to helpless mirth on more than one occasion, but he wasn't a man to settle down with. In fact, she'd received the impression more than once that he didn't want to settle anywhere. He loved the nomadic way of life, whereas Kristin — well, she did eventually want a husband, a home, a family. Did that make her conventional and rather boring? Probably.

She let herself into her mother's house with her key, calling, 'Mum, it's me. Hello-o, I'm back for the night — if that's okay.' There was a moment's silence before Eve's voice came from upstairs. It sounded wobbly.

'Mum?'

'I'm coming.' And Eve appeared on the landing, a handkerchief in her hand as she swiftly wiped what looked like tears away.

Kristin took the stairs two at a time up to her and slipped an arm about her waist. 'What's wrong? Have you hurt yourself? What — ?'

'No, no. I'm okay — really.'

'No, you're not. I can see you're not. You've been crying. Tell me . . . '

'Oh, Kristin — it's Grant.'

'Grant? What about Grant?' Kristin felt her heart give an almighty lurch. Oh God, had he ended things with Eve? Because of Kristin and her actions? She hadn't wanted that. She didn't particularly like him, but . . .

'He's just left.'

Oh no. It was because of her.

'And?'

'It's Stella.'

'Stella? Who's she?' Kristin's brow wrinkled. Should she know who Stella was?

'His ex-wife.'

'Yeah, so?' A tiny pinprick of relief was making itself felt. It wasn't her fault, whatever the problem was.

'Sh-she's back on the scene, and-and . . . '

'And?' Kristin was almost ready to shake her by this time.

'She wants him back, apparently. Oh God, Kristin, I love him. What if he does as she wants? What will I do?' she wailed.

6

'Well — why would he do what she wants?' Kristin asked. 'It certainly looked — the other day — as if he feels the same way about you as you do about him.'

'Well — he says he does, but — '

'In that case,' she soothed, 'what can this-this Stella do?'

Eve shrugged. 'Plenty I would imagine.'

'They are divorced, aren't they?' Because if they weren't, then maybe Eve really did have something to worry about. It could mean that they hadn't been able to bring themselves to make the final break? Which could signify that things weren't really over between them. 'Not just separated?'

'Oh yes, they're divorced.'

Kristin gave a soft sigh of relief.

'They divorced years ago — not long

after the break up.'

'So — why does she suddenly want him back after all this time?'

'Her husband has left her.'

'She re-married?'

'Yes, the man she'd been having the affair with. She and — Nick I think he's called; he's American, so she went to live over there, in New York. They got married over there. He's left her for someone else and she doesn't want to stay on her own so she's come back. She suddenly showed up a couple of days ago.'

'At Grant's house?'

Eve nodded. 'He's told her he's not interested in getting back with her.'

'There you are then — no worries.'

'You'd think so, wouldn't you? But she won't leave him alone. Keeps telephoning, turning up on the doorstep. She says she still loves him — she's even writing him letters.'

'Has he told her about you?'

'He said he has, but — '

'But?'

'Well, it's early days as far as he and I are concerned. He was married to her for quite a long time; they had Daniel. Because of that there'll always be a bond between them. And it does sound as if that's what she's playing on.'

'But he's told you about her; about what she's doing. He wouldn't have done that if he was about to take her back.' Or would he? Was he playing some sort of weird game? Cruelly playing one woman off against the other? Satisfying his ego in some monstrous fashion? After all, it must feel good to have two women so keen to be with you.

But Kristin said none of this to her mother. Instead, she hugged her. Eve looked so desolate, so miserable, that Kristin's heart literally ached for her. She just hoped she was wrong about Grant's possible motives in telling Eve what was happening. If she wasn't, then Eve was heading for a great deal more pain.

'Come on,' she said, giving her

mother a little shake, 'I'll open a bottle of wine and cook us something. Have you eaten yet?'

Eve shook her head. 'I haven't felt like food, to be honest.'

'You've got to eat. It'll make everything seem better. Didn't you used to tell me that when I was upset about something?'

A glimmer of a smile appeared upon her mother's face. 'Yes, I did.'

'There you are then. Mothers always know best.'

A couple of hours later, they'd consumed the meal that Kristin had prepared and drunk a bottle of wine between them. They'd also talked non-stop.

'Daniel and a woman called Sophie visited the camp.'

'Oh yes, Sophie March — they're an item, I believe.'

'Oh?' Kristin stared at her mother. 'He introduced her as a friend.'

'That's not what I've heard and it's not what Grant thinks.'

'What does Grant think?' Kristin made a point of appearing — and sounding — totally unconcerned. Not that she was the least bit bothered about what Daniel Hunter got up to. Why would she be? As far as she was concerned, he and Sophie well and truly deserved each other. Both of them were arrogant, self-centred individuals. They should make a perfect match.

'He thinks they're seeing each other — you know, on a romantic basis. But Daniel flits from one woman to another, apparently; can't seem to settle. I think Grant would like him to find someone — permanently. He can't wait for grandchildren, and he thinks it's more than time Daniel got married and gave him some. Although . . . ' She hesitated, maddeningly. Kristin wanted to urge her on. 'I do get the impression that Grant's not terribly keen on Sophie.'

Kristin chose not to investigate too closely how those words made her feel, or what the sudden quickening of her heartbeat might signify. She might not care for the answer. Instead she asked, 'And how does Daniel feel about his mother suddenly reappearing?'

'According to Grant, he's not impressed. And you can't blame him. She simply up and left him and his father. He was just seventeen at the time of it all. She only ever got in touch at birthdays and Christmases, and sometimes not even then. He's very much on his father's side — or so Grant thinks, anyway. But she is his mother when all's said and done.' And once more, Eve's expression saddened. 'I'm not sure how much influence Daniel has over Grant, but I could imagine he might be able to foster a reconciliation between him and Stella, if he put his mind to it.'

'Does he approve of his father's relationship with you?'

Eve shrugged her shoulders. 'He says he does, according to Grant. But I only met him for the first time the other evening, here.' She eyed Kristin anxiously. 'What did you think of him? He's a forceful personality, and the two of you are very much on a collision course. What did he say when he visited the camp earlier?'

'Oh, just repeated his threat to have us all removed, and then left again with the lovely Sophie in tow. God, she's awful. Even more arrogant than Daniel is, and that's saying something.'

'Be careful, darling,' Eve urged. 'You don't make as much money as he has by being anything other than ruthless. I don't think I'd want to tangle with him.'

★   ★   ★

Kristin returned to the camp the next day to find Richard Millard there once again. 'Hi,' she said. She hoped he wasn't going to be too regular a visitor; and in particular, she hoped he wasn't coming simply to see her.

'Hello, Kristin. It's so good to see

you again. I've brought some food. I was just preparing to hunker down and wait for you.'

Kristin gave a weak smile. 'Oh, don't do that. I can sometimes disappear for hours on end,' she lightly said. 'I was at my mother's; she lives in the village.'

He slanted a glance at her. 'Oh? Are you Eve Lacey's daughter?'

'Yes. Do you know her?'

'Only to say hello to in the village. She did show an interest in the historical society at one point and even attended one of our meetings. Sad to say, she didn't feel it was her thing. Uh — I believe she's friendly with Grant Hunter . . . ' Something flickered in his eyes with that; something that could be speculation. 'How does she feel about you being in opposition to him, so to speak?'

Kristin grimaced wryly. 'Not keen, I have to say.'

'No, I can imagine.' He gave a light laugh.

'Do you know the Hunters?' Had she

asked him this before? She couldn't remember.

'Again — only in passing. I think I'd find them both a little hard to take if you want the truth. Especially Daniel. He always looks so sure of himself. Have you met him?'

'Yes, twice — no, three times. And you're right, he is hard to take. His father's nicer.' Again she grimaced. 'Nice' was hardly the most apt description of Grant. But, in comparison with his high and mighty son, he was considerably more acceptable.

Richard looked almost relieved to hear her view of Daniel. Once again, she hoped he wasn't getting any romantic ideas about her. He really, really wasn't her type. Although if she were being honest, she didn't know who was. She'd only ever had casual relationships with men, not a single one of them coming up to her notion of the sort of man she could love. They'd always been too cool, too amorous, too weak, too strong. She sighed. Was it her? Was she simply too fussy? Whatever the reason, she found it impossible to grow genuinely attached to anyone. Mind you, her current lifestyle didn't make it easy to form any sort of meaningful relationship, being continually on the move, so to speak.

'It's beginning to look as if you and I are kindred spirits,' Richard said.

And that was her cue to take her leave. 'I'll have to get on. I need to put some things away in my tent. Bye, Richard.'

And with that, she hardened her heart against his crestfallen expression and made her escape, steadfastly ignoring his cry of, 'Not for long, I'm sure. I intend to be a very regular visitor, indeed.'

Oh no. And kindred spirits, indeed. They were so dissimilar, they might as well be on different planets. What was that book? Men were from Mars, and women from Venus? Something like that. It couldn't be more true as far as she and Richard were concerned. She just hoped that if she continued to play things cool, he'd take the hint and back off.

And, as if talking about him with Richard had somehow summoned him up, Daniel was the next person to turn up. Without the lovely Sophie, she was pleased to see.

It was Shrimp who alerted her. 'Kristin, someone to see you.'

She was with another couple of women, and the three of them were preparing to reheat some of the food that Richard had brought for supper that evening. They stopped what they were doing and swivelled to see who it could be. One of the women was called Elaine and about the same age as Kristin; she too had joined the group nine months ago — just after Kristin, in fact. It had seemed to create a bond between them; quite a close bond. Kristin gave a sigh. If only she could do the same with a man.

Elaine had told her she'd split up with her husband and had been looking for a different way of life. With no children, there'd been nothing to stop her. 'I wanted a chance,' she'd said, 'to make a difference in the world. To leave some sort of legacy, no matter how small.' Now she softly chuckled, 'Wow! What have you been up to, my girl? He looks good enough to eat. Oh hang on, isn't he the chap who was here the other day with his posh girlfriend? Hey, hey, hey — no girlfriend in sight this time. And, oh my, he looks very determined about something.'

Kristin had looked round too, to see Daniel striding towards them. He must have managed to negotiate the trench because the planks weren't in place across it. Mind you, it would be a simple matter for him to leap over with those long legs of his. Unlike her, who needed to take a good sprint at it.

'What do you want?' she unceremoniously demanded.

'To talk to you,' he equally unceremoniously replied, 'away from here, preferably. The local pub?'

'Go on,' whispered Elaine, at the same time gently nudging her in the ribs. 'Say yes. I dare you. It's about time you had some fun. I'd join you but I think I might not be welcome.'

Kristin ignored her. 'What on earth would we have to say to each other?'

'How about discussing a way to end this impasse? I'll even buy you dinner.' He raised an eyebrow at her stunned expression. 'It would have to be an improvement on whatever you're about to concoct on your campfire.'

'We can prepare some very good meals on the campfire,' she riposted. 'And have.'

Again, Elaine nudged her. 'Say yes. What have you got to lose?' she hissed.

This time Daniel heard her. Mind you, Kristin mused, the whole damned camp probably heard her. Elaine wasn't exactly subtle.

Daniel arched a maddeningly quizzical eyebrow, before giving her a lazy smile. 'Exactly. What have you got to lose?'

Ignoring the quickening of her heartbeat — that smile had been sufficiently beguiling to ensure that she had great trouble in not responding with her own smile — she put a finger to her bottom lip as she gazed skyward, making it look as if she were giving serious consideration to his question. 'Oh, now, let me think. How about my integrity?' Her tone was thick with sarcasm as she met his gaze once more.

Sadly, he didn't seem to notice this. All he did was hold up both hands, palms facing her, as he said, 'I promise I won't compromise that — or anything else.' This last was a barely discernible murmur.

It wasn't too low, however, for Elaine's sharp ears. 'Oh, now that's a shame,' she irrepressibly said.

Kristin glared at her friend before turning back to Daniel. His eyes were gleaming. Which only made him even more handsome. However, Kristin ignored that fact, narrowing her own eyes at him, not bothering to hide her growing suspicion. What was he up to? Trying to charm her into some sort of concession? Well, he wasn't going to succeed. Still, if by agreeing to go out with him she could persuade him to build his wretched houses elsewhere . . . ? It would be worth an evening of argument and aggravation.

'Okay,' she grudgingly agreed.

'Oh, come now,' he bit out, 'let's not show too much enthusiasm. It might just turn my head.'

'I very much doubt I could do that,' she countered. 'It's far too big,' she concluded in an undertone.

'I wouldn't be too sure about that.'

What did that comment mean? Had he heard her final remark? The intriguing gleam had vanished, leaving in its wake an almost devilish look. A minuscule shiver of apprehension shook her. What was she doing, going off alone with him? After all, what did she know about him, when all was said and done? Practically nothing. He could be a serial murderer for all she knew.

Another shiver edged through her.

Trying to ignore her belated bout of misgiving, she said, 'Right. I'll go and change then.'

'Why? You're fine as you are.'

She glanced down at her cut-off jeans and faded T-shirt. 'I don't think Ted at the pub would welcome me in looking like this. As he's told me more than once, he does have his standards.'

Daniel shrugged. 'Please yourself.'

To which comment Kristin softly replied, 'Don't worry, I intend to.'

'But don't be long, I'm starving,' he high-handedly commanded, thus ensuring that Kristin bitterly regretted having agreed to go with him in the first place.

All of which conspired to make her take her time over her toilette — even if it consisted of just a wash in a bowl of cold water. Thank heavens she'd had a bath last night at Eve's, or she might have put him off his food with her smell. She giggled softly. She'd bet the lovely Sophie didn't have to make do with just a bowl.

However, finally she could delay things no longer, and walked out of her tent to a chorus of wolf-whistles from her fellow campaigners, the loudest of them, needless to say, from Elaine.

She'd managed to find a halfway decent skirt she'd forgotten she had with her and a blouse that brought out the colour of her eyes, its boat-shaped neckline showing off her tanned and satin-smooth shoulders. She'd even unearthed a fairly respectable pair of sandals — well, flip flops, to be exact.

'Wow!' called Shrimp. 'That can't be my mate Kristin. How did she manage that in that cramped little tent? A miracle, no less.'

Kristin glanced at Daniel and noted the glint in his eye that told her he was equally impressed. But all he said was a low, 'As I told you once before, you scrub up exceedingly well,' which meant that she began the evening already irritated by him. 'So,' he said, holding held an arm for her to take, 'shall we go? My car's parked in the lane.' He looked doubtful then for the first time. 'Do you think you'll get over the ditch in those?' And he indicated her flimsy footwear.

'Sure. I'll just take them off and jump.'

But Zen was ahead of them, and already carrying the planks of wood to facilitate Kristin's crossing. 'Good luck,' he whispered in her ear. 'Use that sex appeal of yours and get him to call the whole thing off. Just don't go too far; there are limits to what one should have to do in the pursuit of a good cause.'

★ ★ ★

Daniel was driving the Range Rover that she'd seen on their first encounter and which he'd parked in a lay-by in the lane.

'Do you never stop to consider the harm a large, gas-guzzling car like this does to our environment?' she waspishly asked.

'For your information, I'm using a

green fuel. But, aside from that, I don't think a decidedly ancient Ford Fiesta would pull a horse box very well.' His expression was a sardonic one. Kristin said nothing more. There was no shaming this man, evidently.

He parked on the forecourt of the Sun and Slipper pub, one of only two that graced the village high street, and climbed out to walk round and help Kristin down from her seat. However, Kristin, being the independent individual that she was, had pre-empted any offer of help that he might make and was standing waiting for him, an expression of defiance wreathing her face. She detested being treated like a weak little woman. She considered herself every bit the equal of a man; better, in fact, than a lot of them.

Bearing that in mind, she completely disregarded the knowing smile now tugging at Daniel's mouth and strode ahead of him into the pub. Ted, the publican, as always was manning the bar.

'Good evening, Mr Hunter,' he said, before allowing his gaze to move to Kristin. To say he looked surprised to see her with Daniel would be a considerable understatement. Gobsmacked would be a more accurate description. 'Well, Kristin, here's a turn up. What brings you here?'

'Him,' she said, turning her head to look at Daniel.

'Now we aren't going to have any trouble, are we?' He eyed Daniel anxiously. 'You two being on opposite sides of the table, so to speak? Only I know what you lot out at the camp can be like; I read the papers.' His normally genial face was now creased with anxiety.

'No, Ted,' she said, 'not unless he cuts up rough. In which case, I might have to slap him down.' And she gave him a broad and very mischievous grin.

Ted winked at her. 'Cheeky monkey. You don't change, do you?'

'Can you do us a table for two, Ted?' Daniel calmly asked. He didn't look in

114

any way perturbed by the banter of the other two.

'Oh, my, my.' Ted winked again at Kristin. 'Supping with the enemy, eh?'

'You could say that.' Kristin grinned back. 'But as long as he feeds me well, I'd dine with the devil himself.'

'I don't know which I find most offensive, being described as the enemy or the devil,' Daniel retorted. But then he too grinned at Ted.

'Oh, don't you bother about Kristin. I've known her since she was a little thing. She wouldn't hurt a fly. It's all just show.'

'Phew, that's a relief,' Daniel murmured. 'I was beginning to wonder what I'd taken on.' The gaze that raked Kristin then was a hotly smouldering one. 'Mind you, I think I'd manage to cope.'

Kristin felt as if she were about to go up in flames. It was as if he was physically touching her; every part of her.

'Kristin, what are you doing here?'

Kristin swivelled her head. Richard stood just behind her. His expression was one of unbridled outrage, speedily followed by wounded hurt. 'I thought you were at the camp still. If you'd said you wanted to come here, I would have brought you.' The hurt then changed to narrow-eyed suspicion. 'And why are you with-with him?' He practically spat the question at her, his expression darkening forbiddingly.

'Um — Richard, do you know Daniel?' She spoke calmly, attempting to defuse a situation that was threatening to turn ugly. At the same time, she sensed rather than saw the displeasure on Daniel's face.

'Not really, nor do I wish to. So again, Kristin, why are you with him?' Richard's top lip curled into a sneer now. She'd never actually seen anyone do that before. She stared at it, fascinated.

'I offered Kristin dinner if we could talk.' Daniel must have considered it the right time to intervene. 'I thought she might appreciate a meal away from the camp.'

'Excuse me,' Richard said, sounding furious now, 'my mother went to a great deal of trouble sending home-cooked food to the camp. Kristin most certainly doesn't need your dubious offer to ensure that she eats well.'

'Well, in that case I apologise.' Daniel had recognised the situation for what it was — a man attracted to Kristin. He was trying his best, just as Kristin had — in vain, as it turned out — to defuse the situation. 'Um — I'm sorry, I don't know your name.'

'Richard; Richard Millard, president of the Historical and Countryside Protection Society. We're giving our full support to the protest. We, along with Kristin's fellow campaigners, are going to fight you every inch of the way. You can be assured of that, Hunter.'

'I see. Well, that's why Kristin and I are here. To try and work out some sort — '

'Richard, lad,' Ted now interrupted,

slightly nervously it had to be said — clearly, he could see difficulties ahead and was desperately trying to avert them, 'don't get yourself into a state. I don't want any trouble here, as I've already warned Mr Hunter and Kristin.'

'Oh, there won't be any trouble from me,' Richard riposted. 'Not in here. Come along, Kristin, I'll take you back.'

Kristin was taken aback and more than a little vexed. He was treating her as if she were his girlfriend, which she most definitely was not. 'Thanks, Richard, but I want to stay. I'm sure Daniel will take me back to the meadow later.' She made her tone sound as firm as she could, while still remaining friendly. She ended with a conciliatory smile. 'I'll maybe see you at the camp another day. Oh, and do thank your mother for her food. It's very welcome.'

Richard seemed to recognise that he was defeated — for the moment, at least. 'I see. Okay,' he added, sounding fractionally more cordial, 'I'll be off then.' And with no further protest, he left.

Ted stared after him. 'He's a funny one and no mistake. I think he spends too much time with that mother of his. She's just as strange.'

'What about his father?' Kristin asked. She hadn't known the family when she'd lived here, which was strange considering the size of the village. They must have kept themselves very much to themselves.

'Left the pair of 'em years ago. Richard would have been nine or ten. Can't say I blamed him — neither of 'em showed a blind bit of interest in him. Last I heard, he'd divorced Iris and remarried. Started another family, I understand.'

Daniel hadn't uttered a single word throughout this. The only indication of any concern he might be feeling was a deep line of worry between his eyebrows.

It wasn't until they were sitting at a

table for two and had placed their food orders that he said, 'A word of warning. I think you should watch that Millard chap.'

'Richard? Why? He's just trying to help us.'

'Like Ted said, there's something strange about him — obsessive almost, and he's got you in his sights, that's for sure.' He paused then to stare reflectively at her. 'Are you and that other chap — Zen, is it?' She nodded. 'Are you and he — involved?'

'We're close friends, if that's what you mean. Always have been, right from the start. In fact, it was Zen who first got me interested in fighting for our countryside. I met him at a protest meeting about the potential destruction of a strip of ancient woodland, not that far from Bentleigh, actually. Willow Green — do you know it? It's forty miles or so from here — the other side of Birmingham. I joined them there for, oh, a couple of months I suppose, before we moved on.'

'I've heard of it.' He reclined back into his seat, his fingers toying with the stem of his wine glass, watching her through hooded eyes. 'Don't you ever long for an ordinary life? I mean, how old are you?'

'Twenty-four.' Although what business that was of his, she couldn't imagine.

'And not thinking of settling down? Most women are by your age.'

'We didn't come here to discuss my private life.'

He inclined his head in tacit agreement.

'So,' she went on, 'what did you want to talk about, exactly?'

'The meadow, obviously, and how we're going to resolve this impasse between us.'

The waitress placed their food before them. Kristin felt her taste buds salivate. She'd ordered the speciality of the pub: their renowned steak and kidney pie. It smelt delicious. However, she wasn't going to allow it to distract her from the focus of their conversation and the reason why she was here.

'That's easy; you abandon any thoughts of building until the field has been thoroughly examined for any remnants of a battle — or battles.'

'That could take months; years, even.' He sounded exasperated. 'We can't wait that long.'

'Why not?' Kristin raised her gaze to his, her expression one of guileless innocence.

'Because we can't. And it's unnecessary. We've been assured there are no artefacts and the meadow was never a battle site. Look, there's a great deal of money at stake here.'

'Yeah, I know.' Kristin chewed enthusiastically at her food. 'With each house costing over a million pounds. Tell me, how many houses will there be?'

'Only ten. We're aiming to keep it very exclusive. Each will have over an acre of land, some more.'

'Keeping it exclusive, eh?' Kristin

snapped. 'Well you'd have to, wouldn't you? The kind of people who'd buy that sort of house wouldn't want the hoi-polloi as neighbours, now, would they? But, let's see . . . ' She pretended to calculate on her fingers. 'Ten houses at a minimum of a million pounds. They'll make a substantial profit for you and your father. How much would you say to within the nearest million, give or take?'

He ignored that, instead telling her, 'We're also building a number of starter homes. The houses are not just for the wealthy.'

'And that would be fine,' she put in, 'but for the fact that you'll be risking destroying precious things — priceless things, possibly.'

'What do you have against profit making, Kristin? If businesses don't make a decent profit, there would be no such thing as an economy in this country. And who would then pay the taxes that we need to keep everything moving — the schools, the roads, the

National Health Service — to make it possible for people like you to do what you do? You must claim some sort of welfare payment.'

'I don't actually.'

A flicker of curiosity lit his eye. 'So what do you live on?'

'My father, when he died, left me an inheritance. I'm using some of that.'

'And what did he do to make his money?'

Kristin hesitated. 'He ran an engineering business.'

'Profitably, presumably?'

She nodded. She could see where this was going.

'Which you're now living off.'

She said nothing. She'd walked straight into that one.

'What do you think he'd say if he knew what you were spending his hard-earned cash on?'

Kristin slammed her knife and fork down onto the table. 'It's none of your business.'

'Just as it's none of your business

how I plan to make my money.'

'There is a difference. My father didn't want to build over a piece of land that could have relics of our country's history buried in it. He had principles.'

'Rubbish. If he'd had to have done that, he would have. He was a successful businessman too — he would have done whatever it took.'

Kristin stood up, so precipitately that the legs of her chair screeched across the tiled floor. Heads were starting to turn, people beginning to stare, to whisper. She had to get out of here, away from this loathsome man. She didn't want to be associated in any way with him. She began to swiftly walk away.

'Where are you going?'

'Back to the camp. I don't have to listen to this. I'll walk back.'

'Oh no, you won't.'

Kristin ignored that and headed for the exit. Daniel followed her. She heard Ted say, 'Kristin — Mr Hunter?'

'Kristin, it will soon be getting dark,'

Daniel furiously pointed out, at the same time slamming some money onto the bar top.

'You'll need some change, Mr Hunter,' Ted called.

'Keep it,' Daniel responded. 'Look, Kristin, I'm not allowing you to walk alone along that lane. It's not lit.'

'I'll walk where I want.' She was outside by now and she rounded on him. 'I'll do exactly as I want and you can't stop me.'

'You want to make a bet on that?' he savagely bit back.

'You can be sure of that,' she bit straight back.

He reached out and grabbed her by the shoulders. 'You will not walk back — you will not. Do you know, you are the most exasperating woman.'

He pulled her into him so hard that her body struck his — which meant that their faces were only an inch apart. It also meant that she saw the exact second his eyes darkened and his face paled before, in a breath, he was holding her close, his arm around her waist, his one hand behind her head, pulling her in, towards him.

Helpless to resist the onslaught of longing that unexpectedly swamped her, she lifted her face to his, her lips instinctively parting for the kiss she was positive was coming.

'Kristin . . . ' he softly groaned; so softly, she almost didn't hear him.

The small sound, however, was enough to restore her to her senses. 'Let go of me,' she hissed. 'What on earth are you doing?'

He released her instantly, so instantly that she staggered backwards. She stared at him, her eyes wide with horror at what had so nearly happened. He was looking as shocked as she felt — as if the surge of emotion had taken him by surprise as well. His eyes narrowed, forming opaque slits as he watched her. 'Kristin?'

She swung and began to walk away from him, as fast as her trembling legs would let her.

'Oh no you don't. You're coming with me.' And he grabbed hold of her arm, swinging her to face him once more.

'Ouch,' she cried, her arms swinging like the blades of a windmill as she tried to bat his hands away from her. 'Let go, you-you bully. You're hurting me.'

But he resisted her efforts and literally dragged her towards his car, once there opening the passenger door, after which he bodily, and none too gently, lifted her into the passenger seat. He then strode round to the driver's side and climbed into his own seat.

Infuriated by what she deemed his brutal treatment of her, Kristin reached for the door handle. She was getting out — right now. He couldn't stop her.

But he did. She barely had the door open before he leaned across her and slammed it shut again. 'You are not walking back to the field alone. Supposing Millard is lurking somewhere?'

Kristin stared at him, appalled at what he was suggesting. 'Richard? What would he do? He'd see me back.'

'Would he? He looked very angry with you. I wouldn't trust him as far as I could push him.'

Taking unscrupulous advantage of Kristin's stunned silence, he started the engine. Without another word, he gunned the accelerator and took off.

Kristin was stiff with fury at this display of barefaced arrogance. She'd never felt so helpless and it was a feeling she didn't like. She stared out of the window. It was getting dark — just as Daniel had predicted. And there were no lights anywhere along the lane; he was right about that too, damn him. So, although she hated to admit it, he did have a point.

Even so, she couldn't believe that Richard would try and harm her. Was Daniel deliberately instilling fear into her for his own purposes? After all, it wouldn't suit him to have too many people opposing him. And if the historical society joined the protesters, as it was beginning to appear they would . . .

Something occurred to her then. Did Daniel realise how few members it had? Probably not. So could he be thinking that if he could drive a wedge between her and Richard it would stop them collaborating? Yes, that did make some sort of convoluted sense. But was he really that devious? That manipulative? She wouldn't be surprised.

But whatever Daniel thought, they didn't pass anyone on their way back. He eventually pulled up in the gateway to the field. 'Okay, you can get out now,' he said in a grim voice.

'Oh, thank you, my lord,' she sarcastically retaliated, only just stopping herself from touching her forelock in the manner of the vassals of centuries ago. 'Do you think I'll be safe crossing the field on my own? No evil men waiting to molest me? Oh no, silly me, the only evil man's sitting right here, alongside me.'

His face darkened and his eyes turned to ice. But, even so, he didn't retaliate other than to say, 'I'll stay here till you reach the others.'

'Oh, for God's sake. I'm not a child.'

Without giving him the chance to respond to that, as she suspected he might, she pushed the door open and leapt out. The planks were still in place and she could see the other campaigners clustered around the fire, hear their voices as they talked.

She walked towards them, deliberately taking her time. It was a small gesture of defiance, but nonetheless it was defiance. She felt an overwhelming need to demonstrate that she didn't need — or want — him watching over her.

Even so, the vehicle didn't move until she reached them, and then she heard the sound of the engine as it reversed into the gateway, turned and headed back towards the village.

7

Zen was the first one to spot her coming towards them. 'Hi,' he called, 'how did it go? Has he conceded defeat in the face of your irresistible charm and appeal?'

'No,' Kristin muttered, 'anything but. He's determined that the plans are going ahead.'

'I see. So charm didn't work?'

'Nothing would have worked in the face of his overwhelming desire to make money.' She snorted with contempt. 'That's all that matters to him. And-and I doubt he'd recognise charm even if I'd used it.'

'Which you didn't, by the sound of it.' Zen's tone sounded like one of disappointment.

'No.' Kristin looked at him. Despite his cautionary words to her as she'd left him earlier, she found herself wondering now whether he'd actually wanted her to try and seduce Daniel. What would he say if he discovered she could so easily have done just that but had chickened out?

'You argued with him instead.' It wasn't a question; it was a statement — that was how well he knew her.

'Yes,' she admitted sheepishly. That final remark of his had sounded dangerously like criticism. But there was no way she going to crawl and plead with Daniel Hunter. 'Look, it's been a long day and an even more stressful evening. I'm off to bed. Goodnight.'

★   ★   ★

It didn't take long for Richard to fulfil his promise to be a regular visitor to the meadow. He showed up towards the end of the next afternoon, beaming at Kristin and waving a newspaper. It was the *Gazette*. 'Great article and photograph,' he said. 'It'll really get people talking.'

Kristin took it from him and read the front page headline: LOCAL BEAUTY GIVES UP JOB TO TAKE UP FIGHT FOR MEADOW. 'That's a bit misleading. Not true, in fact,' she muttered. 'I gave up my job nine months ago.'

She stared at the photograph. It was of her alone — the last thing she'd wanted. She swallowed and read on. The article repeated word for word all that she'd said, even her disparaging remarks about the local shops not stacking the goods that the newcomers would probably demand. How could she have been so stupid? So contemptuous? She would be a pariah in the village from this time on. And Eve was going to have a fit.

She glanced back at Richard. He was still grinning, clearly immensely pleased with what was written and with her part in it. It was as if the encounter in the pub the evening before had never happened, his antagonistic jealousy over the sight of her and Daniel together obviously forgotten. So much so, it made her wonder whether she'd imagined his vitriol, his air of possessiveness towards her. It was starting to look remarkably like it.

However, for her part, she hadn't been able to forget what had happened. In particular, Daniel's surprising attempt to kiss her, and her equally surprising response. She still couldn't believe it. She'd actually, for a couple of moments, wanted him to kiss her and been more than ready to kiss him back. Her flesh still burned at the memory. Supposing she'd let it go on? How would it have ended? Or had he thought a spot of lovemaking would have her capitulating over the matter of the housing development? Had that been his intention all along? Had that, in fact, been his main reason for asking her out? To seduce her?

She regarded Richard once more, glad of the distraction he offered to her disturbing reflections. He'd brought another large cooking pot, she saw. My, my, his mother had been busy.

'Thank you, Richard,' she said. 'This is very kind of your mother.'

'She enjoys cooking and, frankly, she hasn't much else to do. You'll have to come and meet her. She's been on at me to find myself a girlfriend for years.'

This time she knew she wasn't imagining the meaning in his words — and his eyes. It was time to speak out; to put him straight. 'Um — Richard, I-I'm not your — '

'Kristin — ' It was Elaine, her eyes sparkling with laughter and not a little envy. ' — what is this strange power you seem to have over men that keeps drawing them to you? Can you give me some tips?' She held out a hand to Richard. 'Hello, I'm Elaine. And you are?'

'Richard Millard.'

'Ah yes, the chap from the historical society.'

'The president, actually,' Richard indignantly pointed out.

'Oops, sorry. Mr President, it is then,' Elaine irrepressibly murmured.

Kristin didn't dare look at her; they'd probably both end up laughing and she didn't know how Richard would take that. She would imagine his dignity could be very easily punctured.

'I was just suggesting that Kristin come and meet my mother.' His words were cool now, and his expression had darkened the more Elaine had teased.

Kristin swallowed. She really ought to make it clear that she was not in the running for the position of his girl-friend, but Elaine's presence had put the kibosh on that. No matter how much she wanted to make her feelings — or lack of feelings — plain, she couldn't bring herself to embarrass him in front of Elaine.

But Elaine, as thick-skinned as ever and so totally impervious to the sensitivity of others, winked at Kristin, thus inspiring a feeling of dread about what she was going to come out with next. She didn't disappoint.

'Wow!' she cried. 'That is truly

serious stuff — going home to meet mother.'

And Kristin knew she had to say something right now. Embarrass him or not, it wasn't fair to let him go on believing that she shared his sentiments.

'Oh no, really, I'm no one's girlfriend. I'm what is known as a free spirit, and will continue to be so for the foreseeable future.'

Although she spoke lightly, and with a smile fixed to her face, there was no mistaking Richard's frown of displeasure. But then, in the next instant, the frown vanished and he was chuckling. 'I was only teasing you. You didn't take me seriously, did you? But my mother does want to meet you, if you wouldn't mind, when you've got some spare time. I've told her all about you.'

'Well, I'm not sure.' The very last thing she wanted was to go and meet Richard's mother. It would bestow a significance on their friendship that was totally unmerited. Despite his laughing things off, she had an uncomfortable suspicion that he was indeed viewing her as potential girlfriend material — as his mother could also be if her keen desire to meet Kristin was anything to go by.

But suddenly, she saw a way out. Why hadn't she thought of it before? 'Look, why don't you bring her here? She'd be most welcome and I'm sure she'd be interested in seeing what we've achieved. It would also give everyone an opportunity to thank her for her kindness and generosity.'

Once Richard had left again, visibly gratified by her invitation, she turned to Elaine and admonished, 'Did you have to be quite so outspoken? He's already got enough misguided notions about me without you adding to them.'

Elaine feigned shocked surprise. 'I didn't have to add anything. It's all of his own making.'

★ ★ ★

It took just over twenty-four hours for Richard to turn up again, this time with a woman who couldn't be anyone else but his mother. He was an almost exact replica of her in looks: the same deep-set eyes placed ever-so-slightly too close together; the identical beaky nose; the thin-lipped mouth and sharply protruding front teeth. Even their builds were the same, medium height and bony.

'Kristin, as promised — my mother. Mum, meet Kristin, the leading light of the campaign.'

'Oh, well, I wouldn't say that.' Kristin didn't hesitate in correcting him this time. She didn't want any more misconceptions. 'We all play an equal part. But it's nice to meet you, Mrs Millard.'

'Oh, call me Iris, please. I'm very pleased to make your acquaintance, Kristin. Richard has told me so much about you.'

She held out a hand and when Kristin took it, held on so tightly that, once she was free again, Kristin found herself surreptitiously inspecting her fingers for bruises.

'I — well, we all wanted to thank you for the delicious meals you've been sending us.' She indicated the group of protesters who had all appeared as if at a given signal.

'Well, it's the least I can do. You're doing such good work here. My boy has been so concerned about what is being planned.'

Kristin didn't dare look at Elaine, who was standing close to her now. She must have guessed who had arrived and, Elaine being Elaine, naturally wouldn't want to miss a single word. In fact, it was probably she who had summoned everyone. Kristin just hoped she wouldn't come out with anything embarrassing as she had the day before. To her relief, Elaine stayed silent, although she did hear a tiny gasp as Iris referred to 'my boy'.

'We're hoping that our presence will prevent the building work going ahead, at least for the foreseeable future, but the Hunters do seem very determined,' Kristin told her.

'Huh! Greed, it's all down to greed. I've met plenty of their sort over the years.' She sniffed, thereby signalling her contempt for the two men.

Kristin merely smiled and nodded her agreement with this sentiment.

'Now, tell me, Kristin, I believe you come from the village originally and your mother still lives here? Would I know her?'

'Um, I don't know. Eve Lacey? She lives in Laurel Avenue.'

'Oh, I know it. A very nice part of the village.'

'Yes,' Kristin murmured.

'Richard tells me your mother's not too keen about you doing this sort of thing. She probably wishes you'd find a nice man and settle down, give her some grandchildren.' She smiled ingratiatingly. 'I know I want my boy to do just that.' She smiled fondly at Richard. 'And now he's met you . . . well, it's given me real hope.'

Kristin heard Elaine's smothered gasp at her side and turned a repressive stare her way. She then swung back to Iris and said, 'Oh, you mustn't pin your hopes on me.'

Iris looked surprised by that and darted a swift glance at Richard, who was starting to look distinctly uncomfortable. 'Mum, please . . . '

'You need a nice house to get you off this field,' Iris went on, having, after her first start of surprise, evidently deciding to ignore Kristin's protest, 'I mean, I know you're trying to stop it being spoilt, but there's all these others to do that. A nice little house for two — that's what you need. I mean . . . ' She glanced around then, as if spotting the tents for the first time. 'You surely don't live in one of these, not with your mother having such a nice house nearby?'

'I do, actually.'

'Well, that won't do. My Richard would — '

'Mum,' Richard's tone was a sharp one now, as he took in Kristin's increasingly aghast expression, 'I think you're jumping the gun a bit. It's very early days yet.'

'Quite,' Kristin eagerly put in. 'And I love my life; the freedom of it. No ties.'

'I know, but really, a young woman like you — so pretty. You deserve better. Your mother must think so too. Now — ' She reached out and patted Kristin's hand. ' — you must let Richard bring you for dinner. You can stay the night; we have the room.'

'Oh, well, I wouldn't want to impose.'

'I insist,' Iris said. 'Richard, you must set a date and let me know.' She smiled at Kristin. 'We can have a lovely, cosy chat, get to know each other. You make sure he tells me. Head like a colander, he has. His father was exactly the same.'

Richard did manage to muster up a weak smile at this point. Kristin was aware of a pang of pity for him. No wonder he seemed older than his years — which must be his late twenties; he'd never actually said — living with this domineering woman. It would be enough to prematurely age anyone.

As his mother finally walked away, Richard asked, 'Would you mind coming to visit? She'll nag me until I've fixed something up.'

'I don't know, Richard,' Kristin said, frowning at him. 'If you want the truth, I'm starting to feel pressured. I mean, I don't want her thinking there's something between us when there isn't.' She looked around then. Where was Zen? He could be helping her out. But he was nowhere to be seen. She swung to Elaine, who was looking highly entertained by all of this. 'Have you seen Zen?'

'He went into the village. He needed a few things.'

'Oh, I see.' She faced Richard again. His expression had hardened at her refusal to do as Iris wanted.

'Very well,' he said stiffly. 'In that case, I certainly won't harass you.'

Oh Lord, now she'd offended him. 'I

hardly know you — or your mother, Richard.'

'She won't be best pleased. In fact, she'll be livid, and when my mother's livid, it's best to keep out of her way. I don't know what I'll do.' And he did indeed looked confused; lost, even, and more than a little troubled. It must be because of Iris. She probably bullied him mercilessly, if her performance here was anything to go by.

'Sorry.' And she did genuinely feel sorry for him. But, good grief, he was a grown man. He should stand up to his mother, not bow to her every command. That was why she was like she was, undoubtedly. Because he let her get away with it.

'Kristin?'

Kristin whirled, glad of the interruption, but even more glad when she saw that it was Lizzie who'd spoken, her best friend since high school.

'As you haven't been to see me, or even called, I thought I'd come to you. I wondered if you fancied a walk to the pub? It's such a lovely evening.'

'Oh, Lizzie, yes. That sounds great. Look, I'm sorry, I was going to ring you, but I've been so busy here.'

'That's okay, I can see that. You've done amazingly well to get all this done.' She waved a hand, indicating the camp site. 'But I'm going to drag you away now. A drink at the Sun and Slipper? It's been so long since we've had a good natter.'

A small cough from behind them alerted Kristin to the fact that Richard was still there. She thought he would have followed his mother. She was sure he was supposed to have done.

'Oh, sorry. Lizzie, this is Richard Millard of the historical and — '

'Yes, I know who he is.' She looked directly at him then. 'I've read about you in the *Gazette*. Nice to meet you. I think I've seen you once or twice in the village.'

Richard held out his hand. Lizzie took it with a warm smile. 'It's nice to meet any friend of Kristin's,' he said.

'Look, how about I drive you both to the pub? Save you walking.'

'Uh — ' Kristin cast around wildly for an excuse; any excuse. Then she noticed Iris standing in the entrance to the field, her arms crossed over her flat chest, visibly vexed by her son's tardiness. As Kristin had surmised, he had been expected to follow her. 'What about your mother? She's waiting for you.'

Richard glanced across the field. 'Oh, so she is. She should have brought her own car.' He clicked his tongue in irritation. 'I could easily have walked back later.' He looked back at Kristin, his gaze eager, hopeful. 'I could come along once I've taken her home. Or maybe she would take my car? Yes, that's it. I'll go tell her.'

Kristin looked at Lizzie, her expression one of mute appeal.

Lizzie didn't let her down. She'd always instinctively known when Kristin was in need of her help. It had proved a godsend on more than one occasion in the past. 'You really don't want to spend the evening with us. Trust me. It'll be all girlie talk — you know, frocks, shoes, makeup. Men have no place in that — not unless you wear makeup, that is. You don't, do you?' She peered at him in a comically exaggerated fashion.

Smothering a chuckle, Kristin regarded her friend with bemusement. Those were the last things that she and Lizzie ever talked about. Their respective lives, interests, current events, even politics on a couple of occasions, took precedence over frocks and shoes. Although the topic of boyfriends did occasionally arise, certainly as far as Lizzie went. Mainly because she got through them with the speed of a runaway locomotive, which wasn't surprising the way she looked. Petite, she was only a touch over five feet, blue-eyed, with a perfect heart-shaped face and full lips. She possessed a figure that would rival that of the most glamorous women. Men gravitated to her side like bees towards a rose. Kristin, at five foot six, had always envied her, feeling more often than not like the proverbial cart-horse alongside of her.

Richard's expression now altered dramatically. 'I see. Okay. I know when I'm not wanted.' He looked and sounded like a sulky little boy, even down to the protruding bottom lip. He seemed to alternate between an old man and a schoolboy. No wonder he was confused. He didn't seem to know which role he should stick with.

'It's just that Lizzie and I haven't seen each other in such a long time.' Kristin made every effort to soften her rejection. She hadn't been able to miss the hurt in his eyes. Really, Lizzie could be so blunt at times. Almost another Elaine.

'Well, maybe another time,' he grudgingly agreed.

'Richard,' his mother called, 'come along, do. I can't wait here all night. I've got things to get on with.'

'Oops,' Lizzie chuckled, 'better go.

Mummy's getting cross.'

Kristin closed her eyes in despair. As for Richard, he clearly wasn't sure whether Lizzie was joking or not. 'I can assure you, my mother does not dictate to me.'

'Good for you,' Lizzie cried. 'Atta boy — you tell her.'

Kristin cautiously opened one eye just in time to see Richard stalking away, his back stiff with outrage.

'Oh dear, have I upset him?' Lizzie asked.

'Looks like it. He's a bit touchy, especially where his mother's concerned.' Kristin shielded her eyes then, the better to watch the pair of them climbing into the car before gingerly negotiating the planks across the ditch.

'Well, for heaven's sake, does he always do what she says?'

'I believe so. And take it from me, if you knew her, you'd understand why.'

'Well, what a wimp.'

'She seems to have this bee in her bonnet about him and me becoming a couple, as does he. God knows why either of them would think that. I've certainly not encouraged the idea. Anyway, she's asked me to dinner one evening and to stay the night — so we can get to know each other. Her words, not mine.'

'You're not going, are you? I must say though, he's obviously got the hots for you. You want to watch out.'

'I will, and no, I'm not going. I'd rather have dinner with the devil.' Although, come to think of it, she'd already done that — the night before last. 'He can get any idea of anything like that out of his head. The mere thought of her as my mother-in-law . . . ' She burst out laughing, slightly hysterically it had to be said.

'Come on, let's go. We can talk on the way.' Lizzie took hold of her arm, pulling her towards the gateway.

'I want to get back before dark,' Kristin told her. 'That lane can be a bit scary on your own.'

'Okay.' Lizzie eyed her keenly then.

'So if Richard's not the man for you, who is? Is it still that Zen?' Kristin had mentioned Zen during one of their many phone calls.

'No, we're good friends but it's never really gone beyond that. He's not ready to settle down.'

'Ho, ho, ho. Does that mean you are?'

'Well, if you mean leaving the group and living somewhere permanently, then I suppose I am. I don't want to use up all of my legacy on day-to-day living expenses. So as I refuse to claim any sort of benefit, I've decided I'll shortly need a job.'

'What will you do?'

Kristin shrugged again. 'Don't really know. I know I don't want to go back into an office job, not after the way I've been living for the past few months. I need some sort of challenge. And I don't want to live at home. I thought perhaps I'd buy my own apartment, and to do that I need to keep some of my money back for a deposit.' She stared thoughtfully at the ground for a long moment. 'I don't know whether you've heard, but Mum's got herself involved with Grant Hunter.'

'What? Not the Grant Hunter responsible for the development you're trying to stop?'

Kristin nodded. 'That's the one.'

'Flippin' heck. That's a bit awkward. And no, I hadn't heard. They've kept that quiet.'

'I know.' Lizzie was watching her expectantly now. 'Mum's besotted. And I have to admit, he seems to be too.'

'I can hear a 'but' coming.'

'But he has a son. Daniel.'

'Yeah, now him I have heard about. The local girls are raving about him. A pretty gorgeous specimen by all accounts.'

'You could say that,' Kristin murmured noncommittally.

'Have you met him?' Lizzie cried.

'Mmm. Four times, actually.'

Lizzie couldn't hide her relish now. 'Well, come on, tell all.'

'There's not much to tell. We argued. Pretty fiercely. He's the driving force behind the housing scheme, I'd put money on that. I think Grant would listen to our argument against and maybe think again. Especially if I could get Mum on my side.'

'Never mind all that,' Lizzie said impatiently now. 'What's Daniel like? Come on, spill the beans.'

'You've already said it — he's good-looking, end of story. We had a meal together the evening before last at the Sun and Slipper.'

'Not much to tell? A masterpiece of understatement if ever I heard it,' Lizzie positively chortled. 'Was it just the two of you?'

'Yes.'

'You dark horse you. So?'

'He won't listen to anyone's side of the argument but his own. He's the most infuriating man I've ever met. We ended up having a fight, and-and . . . '

'And what?' Lizzie was practically shrieking by this time.

'He-he tried to kiss me.'

This time, Lizzie did shriek. 'My God!' She covered her mouth with both hands then, just for a second. Her eyes were like saucers staring at Kristin over her fingers. 'He tried to kiss you? But — I heard he was involved with someone else.'

'Yeah, Sophie March. I met her too.'

'And you've kept all this to yourself? Why didn't you ring me? I'm supposed to be your best friend.' Without giving Kristin time to respond to all of this, she went on, 'So what was it like, having him try to kiss you?'

At this point, Kristin paused for reflection. 'Oh, well . . . surprising, I suppose, although he didn't actually do the deed. I came to my senses in time.'

Lizzie's face turned puce at this. 'Surprising? Is that all you can say?' She screamed the words, literally. A couple of birds, thoroughly alarmed by the commotion, erupted from the hedgerow in a mad flutter of wings and feathers, squawking loudly as they passed overhead. 'Okay, let's get this straight. The local heartthrob tries to kiss you. What did he do? Hold you in his arms?' Kristin nodded. 'And all you can say is, it was surprising. Be more explicit, can't you? In fact, the more explicit the better.' Her eyes gleamed avidly.

'That's it. He held me and-and was about to kiss me. More in anger than any sort of passion, I suspect.' She wrinkled her brow. 'I got the distinct impression he'd have been happier slapping me.'

'And what did you do?'

Kristin paused. Should she tell Lizzie she'd wanted him to kiss her? No, she couldn't. 'I got all indignant and he let me go. That's it, really. End of story.'

'Are you crazy?' Lizzie burst out.

'The complete opposite, actually. Sanity won out. After all, why on earth would I want Daniel Hunter kissing me? That would be crazy.'

'Why — ?' Lizzie looked lost for words now.

'It's obvious, isn't it? We're on opposing sides, and-and I didn't want to be in his company for another second, but he — '

'Yes? Yes? He what?'

'He wouldn't let me go. He literally picked me up and threw me into his car.'

'Wow! I like it. A genuine he-man, a real-life alpha male. You don't get many of those to the pound. You lucky so-and-so.'

'Oh, stop it. It was maddening.'

'Maddening, yeah, but did you go with him?' Lizzie's grin was pure lust now.

'I had no choice,' Kristin muttered. 'I opened the door to get out and he slammed it shut again. It seemed easier to stay put.'

Lizzie was speechless again. To have that happen twice in a matter of minutes had to be some sort of record, Kristin decided.

'And, to be truthful, I-I didn't really want to walk back alone; it was getting dark.'

'Well, why would you, when you had a gorgeous man demanding he take you?'

They'd reached the pub by this time and walked inside.

'My treat,' Lizzie insisted.

'Okay, thanks. A shandy, please.'

'Wow! The last of the big spenders. I can afford a glass of wine if you want.'

'No, shandy's fine. Wine goes to my head rather too quickly these days, and if I've got to walk home . . . '

'Okay. Ted,' Lizzie called to the publican, 'a white wine and a shandy, please.'

'Hello again, Kristin.' Ted smiled. 'No Mr Hunter this evening, then? Oh,' he added, glancing beyond her towards the door, 'I spoke too hastily.'

Both Lizzie and Kristin swivelled their heads at that, Lizzie with embarrassing enthusiasm and another soft 'Wow!', Kristin more slowly, and with noticeably more reluctance. And just as she'd feared, there was Daniel, accompanied by the man who'd been with him on that first heated encounter.

159

8

'Damn, damn,' Kristin softly swore.

'Wow!' Lizzie yet again said.

'Will you stop with the wowing?' Kristin hissed. 'He'll hear you.'

Daniel's gaze flicked immediately to Kristin and then moved on to Lizzie. He murmured something to his companion and they began to walk towards the two women.

'They're coming over,' cried Lizzie. 'I bagsie Daniel. The gossip's right; he's absolutely gorgeous.'

'Lizzie, keep your voice down, please,' Kristin softly pleaded.

'Okay, but, my God, he's amazing. Look at those eyes. My legs have turned to jelly. He can try and kiss me any time he wants to, and he won't have to throw me into a car to do it.' Lizzie was practically licking her lips.

'It wasn't in the car,' Kristin murmured.

'Hello, Kristin,' Daniel interrupted. Something flickered in the depths of his eyes.

Oh no, Kristin agonised. *He hasn't heard Lizzie, has he?*

But other than that fleeting glint, there was no other indication that he might have overheard anything. 'How nice to see you again.' Exactly like Richard, it was as if their row of two nights ago had never taken place. His gaze moved to Lizzie. 'Won't you introduce me, Kristin?'

'Sure,' Kristin grudgingly agreed. Lizzie, she noticed from the corner of her eye, was positively preening. How could she? Her best friend was engaged in a battle with this man. 'This is Lizzie, an old friend of mine.'

'Hey, not so old,' Lizzie immediately drawled, speaking to Kristin but not taking her gaze from Daniel.

'I can see that,' he murmured appreciatively before turning, with what

Kristin considered a great deal of reluctance, to say to her, 'This is Rex.'

'We've already met,' Kristin muttered.

'Of course you have. How could I have forgotten our first interesting encounter?'

And just as had happened then, Rex's gaze greedily devoured her. She glowered at him, to no effect. All he did was grin rakishly and say, 'You all but fell at my feet as I recall. Not that I'm complaining.'

Kristin felt, rather than saw, Lizzie's quizzical look. Her cheeks flamed. Daniel noticed her embarrassment and, to his credit, said curtly, 'Kristin is most definitely not a woman to throw herself at any man's feet. I can testify to that,' he concluded drily.

She refused to rise to that gibe. He was deliberately goading her; trying to make her lose control again. Why? To make a fool of herself in front of Lizzie and Rex? Well, if that was his game, it wasn't going to work. She was going to treat him with coolness and disdain; demonstrate unequivocally, that she was above such juvenile tactics.

It was at that point that Ted placed their drinks on the bar. 'I'll get those, Ted,' Daniel said, 'and two whiskies for my friend and me, please.'

Not wanting to be beholden to Daniel Hunter in any way, Kristin began to refuse his gesture. But Lizzie, guessing what she was about to do, hastily said, 'Thank you, and would you like to join us?' She then slanted a provocative look at Kristin and asked, 'That's okay, isn't it?'

Which placed Kristin in an almost impossible position. Because how could she refuse with Daniel and Rex both listening? 'S'pose so,' she muttered ungraciously. However, she couldn't resist quietly adding, 'I thought this was to be a girlie evening?'

'Oh, don't be such a killjoy,' Lizzie whispered as they started to make their way to a nearby empty table. 'We can do that another time. I'm not throwing this opportunity away.'

Kristin didn't need to ask 'what opportunity?'. She knew only too well. She was prevented from saying anything further anyway by Daniel and Rex taking their seats on the opposite side of the table. So instead, she asked, 'Where's Sonya this evening?' She then took a large mouthful of her shandy, hoping its alcoholic after-effects would render the evening and the company more palatable. Sadly, it didn't. The only thing that happened was that she swallowed it too quickly and, inevitably, it went down the wrong way, with the result that she began to choke, then cough, with embarrassing gusto.

'Whoa,' Lizzie said, 'take it easy,' before starting to energetically thump her on the back.

Kristin didn't dare look to see what Daniel and Rex were making of it all. Eventually, she pulled herself together and said slightly breathlessly, 'Sorry. It went down the wrong way.'

Daniel made no comment on that. He merely said, 'It's Sophie, not Sonya,' but his level gaze told her that he knew she'd deliberately got the name wrong again. 'And she's at home, I would imagine. She doesn't make a habit of telling me where she's going and who with.'

'Oh?' Surprise made her careless. 'I thought . . . '

Daniel raised an eyebrow in anticipation of whatever was coming next, although she had a strong suspicion he knew. 'You thought what?'

'Um, well, that you two were you know, involved.' She groaned silently. So much for her intention to be cool and disinterested in him. Now he'd think she cared what he and Sophie got up to. Which, of course, she didn't.

And just as she'd expected, that increasingly familiar gleam appeared within Daniel's eye. 'Involved in what?' he took a mouthful of his own drink, managing to not swallow it the wrong way.

'Nothing. I was obviously wrong.' He was being deliberately evasive.

A smile tugged at the corners of his mouth. He knew what she was thinking. And he was making no effort to hide his enjoyment of her discomfort. He also had no intention of enlightening her about the state of his and Sophie's relationship. Not that she gave a toss, in any case.

'So,' Rex said, 'how are things out at the ranch?'

'If you mean the camp, they're fine. Why wouldn't they be?'

'Well, I drove past yesterday and it all looked a bit piecemeal, to say the least. If we wanted to get the bulldozers in, I can't see much to stop us.'

'I think the trench inside of the gateway might,' she sharply retaliated.

'Oh, I doubt that. Have you seen some of those bulldozers?' He cocked his head to one side. 'Believe me, if Daniel wanted to gain entry, then he would. A pathetic little trench wouldn't stop him.'

'Rex.' Daniel's tone was a warning one.

Kristin looked from one to the other. That sounded as if Daniel was deliberately holding back. Why?

'Um, Daniel,' Lizzie said, 'I'm curious. What are your plans, exactly? I'm sure Kristin and her friends would appreciate knowing.'

'I'm sure they would, which is why I'm not telling.' There was a cold, calculating look to him now. 'I'd rather surprise them. Makes life more . . . exciting, shall we say?'

Kristin took another gulp of her shandy. Was that his intention, to catch them unawares? To allow them no time to mount a defence? It would seem probable and would be absolutely typical of him. The sneaky —

'Careful with that,' he unexpectedly cautioned. 'We don't want it going the wrong way again. It seems to be an unfortunate habit of yours.'

'Why don't you mind your own business?' she snapped. He was referring to the dinner party at Eve's when she'd almost choked on her drink then as well. Only that time, she'd managed to control things in a more dignified manner.

'That's precisely what I am doing.'

'So, why don't you just move your machinery in, if Rex is correct and modern-day bulldozers would have no problem? You could do it at any time. Why not simply annihilate our defences and to hell with people's safety?'

'There you have it. People's safety. I'd rather we came to a reasonable agreement about it all.'

'That's not going to happen, which means you'll be waiting a hell of a long time. So, it looks like it's bulldoze or lose.' Her patience expired at that point. 'Come on, Lizzie, I've finished. Let's go. We'll try the Slug and Lettuce. The company might prove more congenial.'

'Okay.' Lizzie nervously regarded her friend's stormy expression. She did, however, manage an apologetic smile at the two men as she got to her feet. 'Sorry.'

'That's okay.' Rex grinned up at them. It was to Kristin that he spoke, however. 'Can't stand any sort of opposition then? Even a verbal one?'

'I can, yes,' Kristin bit back, 'if it's reasonable opposition, not veiled threats to remove us regardless.'

'I wouldn't threaten anyone,' Daniel grimly put in, 'and I'm trying my utmost to be reasonable — under a great deal of provocation, I have to say.'

But Kristin wasn't listening. She was well on her way out of the pub with Lizzie meekly and silently following.

'Did you see his face?' snorted Kristin.

'Whose?'

'Daniel's, of course. You can see he's not used to women walking out on him. It will do him the world of good.'

★ ★ ★

With all that had taken place, Kristin and Lizzie being forced, in Kristin's opinion, to leave one pub and walk to another at the far end of the village, darkness had fallen by the time they eventually left the Slug and Lettuce.

'Are you going to be okay walking back in the dark?' Lizzie anxiously enquired. 'Maybe it would be better to go to your mum's for the night.'

'No. She'll have read the *Gazette* by now and I know she'll be furious at what I said. I can't face the inevitable row, and she's probably out with Grant, in any case. And if they're both there, then he's the last person I want to tangle with. I've had more than enough of the Hunters and their affairs for one evening.'

'But if she's out, you have a key, don't you?'

'Yes, but I've left it in the tent.'

'Well, you could try. Okay, you'd have to wait to be let in, but that would be better than that lane on your own in the dark.'

'Mmm, maybe you're right. I'll try, but if he's there . . . '

But the question didn't arise, because

as she'd expected there was no response to her ringing of the bell. Lizzie regarded her with even more anxiety then. 'Tell you what, come back with me and I'll drive you.'

'No. I'm a grown woman, Lizzie. I'm perfectly capable of getting myself back. Anyway, you've had too much to drink to risk driving.'

'But you said you didn't want to walk back alone this late.'

'If I get a move on, it'll only take me fifteen minutes max.'

★   ★   ★

So that was what she did, and all was well until she reached the part of the lane that was bordered by rows of lofty trees and thick hedgerows, the branches of the trees interweaving tightly over-head to form a solid canopy. It effectively blocked out any moonlight, in the process rendering the road inky black. Her eyes swiftly adjusted to it, but still, it was creepy.

An owl hooted in some branches high above her, intensifying her sense of unease. Something rustled in the hedgerow nearby. She shivered and quickened her step, muttering to herself, 'There's nothing to be scared of; nothing at all. It's just an animal.'

This was Daniel Hunter's fault. He'd inspired the fear with his refusal to allow her to walk the other evening. Till then, she'd never suffered a second's anxiety about walking alone at night.

It was that precise second when she heard what sounded like a footstep, and a fairly softly trodden one at that, somewhere behind her. In the field beyond the hedge, maybe? Next, something cracked, as if someone had trodden on a fallen branch. That was no animal; it sounded much larger. Large enough to be human.

She whirled and peered through the darkness.

'Who's there? Lizzie — is it you?'

Although why on earth she should think it might be Lizzie creeping up on her, she didn't know. She waited a moment or two and upon hearing nothing else, she put it down to her at times over-fertile imagination and set off again, even faster.

She'd only been going for a couple of minutes when she heard the identical sounds once more. It wasn't her imagination. Someone was there — tracking her.

Panic, tinged with anger, surged through her then. 'Who's there?' she shouted. 'Show yourself. I know some-one's there. Who is it? If this is some sort of joke, it's not funny.'

Nothing moved. Whoever it was clearly didn't want to be seen and perhaps recognised.

Kristin didn't wait any longer. She turned and began to run. Fortunately she was wearing trainers on her feet, so there was nothing to impede her headlong dash. For a moment or two the footsteps were even more distinct, light and fast, and they were keeping pace with her. But then they began to slow, as if whoever it was was tiring. Even when everything fell silent once again, she didn't stop. She kept going, refusing to look back. She wanted nothing to slow her, in case it was all part of a plan. Fall silent, still, thereby lulling her into a false sense of security, and then close in for the kill. Her breath began to sob through her parted lips, erupting in painful gasps. Her side began to hurt.

Then, just as she thought that she wouldn't be able to keep running for much longer, she heard the sounds of a car approaching. 'Oh, thank God,' she breathed. 'Thank you.'

She stopped and swung to face the oncoming vehicle. She could see its headlights cutting a bright swath through the darkness of the night. It was getting nearer. She began to wave her arms. 'Stop, please!'

It did, and she instantly recognised the vehicle. It was Daniel's Range Rover. It skidded to a halt in a screech of brakes and Daniel leapt out. He didn't hesitate; he ran to her.

'Kristin, what's wrong?'

She was panting too much to speak at first. Then she managed to gasp, 'Someone . . . someone . . . '

'Yes?' he demanded impatiently.

'Someone was following me.' She got the words out this time as her heartbeat calmed and her breathing gradually slowed. 'I'm sure . . . ' She was bent double now, hands on her knees, fighting for control.

Daniel's skin paled as he ground the words out, 'My God!' He placed both hands on her arms and gently lifted her upright. 'Tell me what happened. Exactly.'

'I-I heard footsteps, a branch cracking — beyond the hedge I thought. Someone was there, somewhere in the field . . . keeping up with me.'

He frowned. 'Wait there. Don't move. There's a gateway. I'll go back and check the field.' He strode back the way he'd come, his long, powerful legs covering the ground much faster than she could. He was gone for what seemed like several minutes while her thoughts ran riot.

Supposing whoever it was had attacked him and intended to come for her? Should she go and look? She began to walk, her entire body shaking with fear, only to turn a corner and almost bump into him.

'I couldn't see anything or anyone. If there was someone there, whoever it was has gone. There was a break in the hedgerow, as if someone had stood there. Some branches had been snapped off. Are you sure you didn't see anyone — anyone at all?'

'No. It was too dark.' She wrapped her arms about herself, trying to contain the shaking that was suddenly threatening to tear her apart. But if anything, her shudders intensified. 'S-someone was-was there, I know it. I could feel it. Wh-what could he want?'

'You're assuming it was a man?'

'Well, I'm sure a woman wouldn't do such a thing.' Her eyes began to sting with tears. Despising herself for her girly weakness, and in front of Daniel of all people, she angrily dashed them away.

His expression softened and his eyes warmed. 'Come here. You're shaken, and no wonder. But I did warn you about walking alone along this lane. It was probably an animal foraging. A badger perhaps, or a fox. There must be quite a few around here.' He reached out and pulled her in to him.

Kristin didn't argue. Mainly because it felt the most natural thing in the world to be held by him. To know she was safe, protected.

He slid his arms around her and pulled her closer; their bodies touched all the way down. Every one of her nerve endings began to tingle as, helpless to resist, she raised her head and gazed up at him. She widened her eyes and parted her lips. She licked them, trying to ease their sudden dryness.

Daniel's face darkened as he stared down at her. 'Oh God, Kristin,' he groaned, 'don't look at me like that.' As if he couldn't help himself, he lowered his head towards her, until their mouths were only an inch apart. He stared at her then from beneath lowered lids, his gaze a smouldering one.

Kristin couldn't move.

His arms tightened yet again about her, pulling her so close she could feel every hard muscle of him. Her arms slid up his chest, her fingers entwining at the back of his neck. She wanted him to kiss her; wanted him.

But then — what the hell was she doing? And with Daniel Grant of all people? She pulled away jerkily, instinctively, placing a gap of several inches between them.

Something else occurred to her then. Something that really did scare her. She stared up at him, not with want this time, but with a growing sensation of dread. 'What were you doing, driving along the lane at this particular time? Bit of a coincidence, isn't it, you showing up? What exactly are you up to?'

9

'What?' He looked startled and then, almost immediately, puzzled. 'What the blazes are you talking about? Just a minute.' His gaze darkened. 'Are you accusing me of something? Of what? Of following you?' Sheer anger blazed at her then, as his fists clenched into tight balls.

Could it have been him? was all Kristin could think, despite his show of fury. Could that simply be an act? Could he have followed her on foot, deliberately terrified her, then silently returned to his car to drive up and pretend to rescue her? He'd already demonstrated how fast he could move, and there were one or two very conveniently placed gateways, as he'd clearly known, leading into the various fields that lined the road where he could have left the vehicle and then, hidden by the high hedges, stalked her. As she'd already wondered once before, could he have hoped that by making love to her he'd persuade her to leave the field, believing she'd in turn persuade her co-protesters to do the same? And was he hoping now that frightening her would achieve the same thing? It did make some sort of crazy sense.

'Well, someone was,' she shouted, 'and you turned up just at the right moment to rescue me.'

His mouth twisted. 'What — I left the car somewhere, pursued you on foot, returned to the car, and drove here? Why would I do such a thing?' He stared at her, eyes narrowed. 'Do you really think I'm capable of deliberately setting out to frighten you? Why? Why the hell would I do that?'

She shrugged. 'You work it out.'

'Why would I want to frighten you out of your wits and then try and kiss you — ? Oh.' She watched as enlightenment dawned. 'Of course, I get it. I scare the hell out of you, in order to kiss you by way of comfort. Then, having softened you up, persuade you to remove your camp from the field, so leaving it free for us. What a terrific opinion you must have of me. Thanks, Kristin.'

Kristin said nothing. The way he was putting it, it did sound preposterous.

'You really think I'm that devious, that cold blooded, that manipulative?'

Still Kristin didn't respond. She couldn't; words had failed her. Mainly because her heart was hammering so hard she was on the verge of passing out.

'Well, I'll take that as a yes, shall I?' he growled. 'In which case, I'll leave you to walk back. Leave you to the mercies of your . . . what? Stalker? If you believe it was me, I won't bother you any longer. You know where I am now and within seconds I'll be gone. Hey, you can even watch me drive away — just to make sure I've really gone.' But he made no move to return to his car. He simply stood, hands on hips, the very picture of arrogant self-possession, watching her, her every change of expression. So doubtless he noted the flash of fear; of dread at being left here alone in the dark. 'Oh, get into the car. I'll take you back to the blasted field.' Even more furious now, whether with her or himself for weakening, she couldn't have said, he strode back to the Range Rover.

But Kristin wasn't about to meekly submit to his will. She'd rather risk life and limb than climb into that vehicle with him, and give in. 'I'll walk, thanks,' she muttered — slightly shakily, it had to be said.

He rounded on her instantly. Startled, she flinched away from him. He looked ready to throttle her. His eyes were blazing; his hands, once again clenched into fists, were raised menacingly. 'Hellfire! You are the most maddeningly stubborn woman it's ever been my misfortune to meet.'

'Me?' she furiously retaliated. 'Stubborn? Tell me, who is it who refuses to change his mind about destroying precious fifteenth-century artefacts? Huh? Not me.'

'Kristin,' he sighed wearily, his anger apparently extinguished in a split second, 'we've taken advice — professional advice — and the general consensus is that the meadow is not a battle site; was never a battle site. Not at any time. How often do I have to say it before you'll believe me?'

'That's not what the historical society says.'

'Oh,' he snorted scathingly, 'and they're the experts, are they? You know my opinion of them, of Millard in particular.'

'Richard is a decent, caring man. You could take a leaf from his book.'

'Oh, I will — when hell has the first snowfall. Look, I'm not leaving you to walk back and be possibly attacked by some nutter on the loose. Now, get into the car — or, by God, I'll pick you up and heave you in again.'

Looking at him, Kristin was in no doubt that he meant every word. He'd done exactly that the last time she'd tried to refuse his offer to take her back. So, grudgingly, and all the while muttering to herself about 'tyrants and greedy capitalists', she did as he said. Neither of them spoke another word until they reached the entrance to the field. He then sat, arms folded across his chest, frowning darkly through the windscreen, while Kristin scrambled down from her seat. After which, without another word, he drove away.

Kristin watched him go, feeling more miserable than she'd ever felt in her entire life. No wonder he was so angry with her. Her and her big mouth. She'd more or less accused him of stalking her, and such crazy and completely unfounded accusations weren't going to help the campaigners' case. Far from it, in fact. For not only had she probably alienated half the village by what she'd so heedlessly said in her newspaper interview, she'd also totally infuriated him, with the result that he'd be even more determined to go ahead with his plans.

Why did she never learn?

There were far more effective ways of getting a man to do as she wanted. He was clearly attracted to her — otherwise why try to kiss her? Why didn't she simply utilise that? Zen believed she should, although he hadn't actually put it into words.

Oh God, she groaned, could she really be considering sinking that low? Practically prostituting herself? No, she couldn't; she wouldn't. That wasn't her way. She had to win this battle by fair means. Nothing else would do.

She was halfway across the field when her mobile phone rang. It was Lizzie. 'Are you back okay?'

'Yeah, although — '

'I bumped into Daniel after you left. He asked where you were, so I told him you were walking back. He was furious,

Kristin. He went off muttering what sounded like 'stubborn bloody woman'. Anyway, he headed back towards his car and then took off like a vampire fleeing from the break of day — '

'Oh no,' Kristin wailed. 'Oh God . . . '
He'd followed her to make sure she got safely back. And she'd . . . she'd . . .

'What? What's the matter? Didn't he catch you up? Because that's obviously what he rushed off to do.'

'Oh, he caught me up all right.'

'So what's wrong?'

'Oh, Lizzie. Just before he turned up I'd heard footsteps somewhere in the field that runs alongside the lane — on the other side of the hedge, I thought — tracking me. Well, it scared me half to death. I'd started to run when I heard a car coming up behind me, so I flagged it down. It was Daniel.'

'Yes, so?'

'He stopped and got out. I told him what had happened, but then . . . ' Her words petered out as her abject misery and guilt overwhelmed her.

'For heaven's sake, Kristin, spit it out. What did you do?'

'I more or less accused him of stalking me.'

'You didn't.' Lizzie sounded genuinely shocked. 'He wasn't on foot, so how — ?'

'I know,' Kristin wailed, 'but I thought that maybe he'd left the car in a convenient place, followed me and then gone back to it, so he could drive up and rescue me.'

'Why would he do that?'

'To scare me; drive me and, therefore, the others away. Oh Lord, what have I done? It sounds absolutely ridiculous now I've put it into words, doesn't it?'

'Yes, and you've made everything a hundred — no, a thousand times worse, I would say. Honestly, Kristin, how could you even think such a thing, let alone put it into words?'

★ ★ ★

Kristin woke late. Her sleep had been punctuated by disturbing dreams of a man who kept his face covered, following her wherever she went. She eventually crawled from her tent to stand blinking in the mid-morning sunshine, yawning and rubbing her eyes.

'Hey.' It was Elaine. 'Last night must have been a good one. You look terrible.'

'Gee, thanks a bunch.'

'Kristin, you look awful.' This was Zen. 'I heard you'd gone to the pub. One too many, was it?'

'No,' she snapped, 'and thanks both of you. You've really made me feel better. It just turned out to be not a very good evening, that's all.' She debated telling them what had happened to her on the way back here, but then thought better of it. It could all have been in her head, the darkness of the lane making her edgy, whipping up her imagination. Still, maybe a question or two wouldn't hurt. 'Have either of you noticed anyone hanging around?'

Zen stared at her. 'Around the camp?'

She nodded. 'Or in the lane?'

'No. Well, there's that Millard bloke; he always seems to be turning up.'

'Yes, I know, but apart from him.'

'No, but he certainly hangs around a lot and he does watch you all the time. Why do you ask?'

'I can tell you why Richard hangs around,' Elaine butted in. 'He's besotted with her; anyone can see that.'

Which set Kristin thinking. Besotted enough to stalk her?

He'd known she and Lizzie were going to the pub and that they were going to walk there — which meant she'd most likely have to walk back alone. Then there was the fact that he hadn't been at all pleased when he wasn't invited too. Add to all of that his extreme reaction when he'd found her and Daniel together. Could he have been checking up on her, wanting to know what she was up to? But how would following her when she was alone have shown him that, and why wouldn't he have answered her when she called out? He must have known she was frightened; heard it in her voice.

No, it didn't make sense for it to be him. He wouldn't want to scare her away, if that was the motive. If he was besotted, as Elaine had said, he'd want her to stay. And, if the truth be known, she still wasn't absolutely sure that there had actually been anyone there — not really. As Daniel had pointed out, it could have been an animal engaged in a spot of nocturnal foraging — a fox, a badger. And the break that Daniel had found in the hedgerow could have been made at any time, by anyone.

Oh, this was ridiculous. 'Forget it, I'm just being silly,' she told the other two.

Nervously, Kristin let herself into the house; she was fully expecting a severe telling-off from Eve about the article in the *Gazette*, and the remarks she'd made. However, her apprehension wasn't so great that she could ignore her desperate need for a bath and a decent home-cooked meal.

But unexpectedly, the sight that met her gaze wasn't one of a furious woman, all guns blazing, but that of her mother standing, seemingly oblivious to anything else, staring intently at herself in the hall mirror, twisting this way and that as she did so.

'Mum, what are you doing?'

'Have I put on weight?'

Kristin eyed her. 'No, I don't think so. You look great. You've always had a good figure.'

'So I don't look mumsy, dull?'

'No, of course you don't. What's brought this on?' She walked to Eve and, placing both hands on her mother's shoulders, swung her to face her. 'Tell me.'

'Stella.'

Oh no. What now? 'What's she been doing?'

'Don't ask.'

'No, come on, tell me.'

'Well, Grant took me out for a meal last night and-and who should walk in to the restaurant but Stella and a friend.'

'So?'

'So she kept staring at me. I felt so uncomfortable, Grant had to change seats with me in the end so that my back was to her. But then, half an hour ago . . . ' Eve stopped talking and tears filled her eyes. 'Sh-she turned up here, at the door.'

'She didn't. The cheek!' Kristin gasped. 'What did she want?'

'To tell me to leave Grant alone. That he wants her, but doesn't want to hurt me.'

'You didn't believe her, did you?'

'I don't know. Maybe she's right.' A solitary tear spilled over and ran down Eve's cheek. She dashed it away. 'Sh-she then said that she'd left him because of his . . . affairs.' Eve's voice broke. She pressed one hand to her lips.

It was trembling. 'That's why she had her affair. He drove her to it. She said that he'll get bored with me and leave me; if not for her, then for someone else.' Eve was openly weeping now, the tears unstoppable.

'Oh, Mum.' Kristin hugged her tightly. 'He wouldn't be with you if he didn't want to be. She's just jealous and sticking the knife in. She's obviously trying to break you up. Don't let her.'

'But you haven't seen her,' Eve wailed. 'She's so slim, so lovely, so glamorous, so utterly perfect. Why would he stay with me when he could have her back again? He won't, will he? He'll leave me, just like she said. She's right, I am ordinary, He could have anyone.' The sobs intensified.

'No.' Kristin gave her mother a little shake. 'From what I've seen, he feels the same way about you as you do about him.' She prayed she was right. 'And-and you're lovely, too.'

Eve regarded her daughter. The tears had slowed, but a frown of uncertainty now creased her brow.

'Listen to me,' Kristin went on. 'I might not like Grant for what he's trying to do to the village, but I'm convinced he's genuine about you. It's written all over him.'

'Oh, darling.' Eve dropped a kiss onto her daughter's face. 'You've made me feel so much better.'

The relief that Kristin felt then at the lack of any sort of criticism over her outspoken remarks in the newspaper was overwhelming. Of course, it could well come later, when Eve had put her worries over Stella to one side, but she'd cope with that when it happened. For now, she'd bask in the unusually good relations she and her mother were enjoying.

'Good,' she cried, 'so forget all about utterly-perfect Stella. Come on, is it too early for a glass of wine?'

And it wasn't just Eve who needed the boost that a dose of alcohol would provide. For, truth to tell, Kristin was nowhere near as confident as she'd sounded with her reassurances to her mother. For all she knew, Grant could be considering going back to Stella — and however would Eve cope with that?

★   ★   ★

Kristin spent the rest of the day with her mother, catching up on the news and gossip. In fact, she felt closer to Eve than she'd felt in a long time. Maybe because, for once, Eve had let her guard down and revealed her emotional side, her vulnerability. It wasn't something she did very often, seemingly feeling a need to hide her feelings from her daughter. Well, from most people, actually. Kristin's father had been the only one to really know Eve, and he'd known her inside and out.

She wondered then if Eve was also hiding her emotions from Grant, and he didn't really know how she felt about him. Maybe Kristin ought to suggest she tell him. But then again, maybe not.

Eve might not appreciate being told what to do by a daughter who, let's face it, hadn't been a raving success herself in the love stakes. In fact, she'd never been in love, not with any of the men she'd gone out with. Which, of course, meant that her relationships had never lasted very long. She often wondered if she'd recognise the emotion if it stepped up and slapped her in the face.

It was eight o'clock before she eventually left. There'd been no mention of the troublesome newspaper article. Maybe Eve hadn't read it. Instead, mother and daughter had enjoyed an early supper together, and Eve had even asked her to stay the night. But Grant was coming over and she knew her mother wished to discuss Stella and get his thoughts about her visit. Eve also needed reassurances from him that Stella's words about his affairs weren't true. Or, at least, his reasons for them if they were true.

'No, I don't want to play gooseberry.'

'Darling, you wouldn't be. Despite

your differences, Grant likes you.'

'Mmm, wish I could say the same for his son. Whenever we meet, all we seem to do is argue. He's so arrogant, Mum; wants everything his own way.' Whatever it was that Daniel felt for her, it most certainly wasn't liking.

Eve was looking amused by this.

'What?'

'Well, darling, you can seem a teeny bit that way at times too.'

Kristin left, laughingly denying that she was anything like Daniel, but inwardly conceding that Eve might have a point.

But that wasn't the end of the evening, not by a long shot.

She was walking through the village, Eve's house being situated on the opposite side to the endangered meadow, when to her dismay she saw Daniel and Sophie sitting at a table outside of the pub, enjoying a drink in the evening sunshine.

10

Kristin's heartbeat quickened. Daniel was the last person she wanted to see. Maybe she could nip across the road before they spotted her — take cover behind the parked cars on the other side. But she'd left it too late. Sophie's disdainful tones reached her all too clearly.

'Oh, good Lord, it's our eager little campaigner. They must have let her out for the evening.'

Daniel swivelled his head to look at Kristin, and judging by the expression that smouldered within his eyes, he hadn't forgiven — or forgotten — her implied accusations of the evening before. Not for anything would she appear to be running away, though, so she carried on towards them, all the while trying to look unconcerned by this unexpected and completely unwanted encounter.

'Hello,' she quietly said upon reaching them, giving no sign that she'd heard Sophie's disparaging remarks. She wanted to apologise to Daniel, admit she'd got things wrong about him and the stalking, but she was damned if she was going to do it in front of Sophie.

But fortune for once smiled upon her, because Sophie picked up their empty glasses and asked, 'Same again, darling?' before walking off to leave them alone.

Daniel didn't speak for a long, long moment, before, with a grim smile, he said, 'I'm sure you'll understand if I don't ask you to join us. Wouldn't want you to think it was some sort of twisted attempt at stalking you again.'

Kristin looked down at him. He wasn't even going to ask her to sit down, although there was a third chair at the table. Instead, he simply leaned back in his seat and stretched his legs out in front of him, crossing them at the ankles, after which he folded his arms across his chest, all the while staring at her, obviously waiting for her to speak.

She obliged. 'Um, I-I was hoping I'd see you. I spoke to Lizzie last night and she told me she'd bumped into you and that she'd said I was walking home alone.' She swallowed nervously. His expression was a formidable one; unforgiving. 'She then said that you went off to find me, to-to . . . '

His one eyebrow lifted. 'Yes? To-to —?'

Normally, she would have made some snappy reply to his sarcastic mimicry. But, deciding that might not be the best way forward, she said, 'To pick me up and take me back, she presumed.'

'She presumed right. And, in the event, it was a good thing that I did. Oh no, that's wrong. Sorry.' His smile was an ironic one. 'You believed it was me following you, didn't you? That it was all part of some evil plan I'd been hatching.'

'No, I didn't — not really. I'm sorry. It was an awful thing to imply.'

'Yes, it was.' With a jerk of his head, presumably towards Sophie who was still inside the pub, he said, 'As you can see, I don't need to stalk unwilling women. There are more than enough only too eager for my company — although you did seem only too ready to fall into my arms, as I recall.' His smile this time was a knowing one.

'Oh — ' The colour flew into Kristin's face. ' — you despicable, arrogant — '

'Oh, please, don't stop there. I'm sure you can come up with a few even more insulting adjectives to define me.'

'Do you know, I can't really be bothered. You're not worth the mental effort.'

The smile fled as his mouth hardened and compressed. His eyes transformed themselves into chips of silver ice. 'Well, maybe that's just as well, because here comes Sophie with my drink. So I'll bid you good evening, Kristin. Oh, by the way, look out for the bulldozers in the next day or so. Because my patience is running out, I'm afraid.' And on that unmistakable threat, he took the glass from Sophie, murmuring, 'Kristin's just going, sadly.'

'Well in that case, let's not hold you up.' Sophie looked directly at Kristin, her expression one of complacent self-satisfaction. 'I wouldn't want anyone I know to see me consorting with the local riffraff.' And she laughed out loud.

Kristin was forced to take a long, deep breath and stifle the overpowering urge to put her hands round both their necks and throttle them. Instead, she swallowed the angry words that were hovering on her tongue and walked away. Sophie's laughter followed her all the way down the road. Hateful, the two of them. She wouldn't care if she never saw either of them again.

But, oh Lord, did they deserve each other? She just hoped they'd be very happy together. But one thing worried her, deeply. Daniel had just said that the bulldozers would be arriving. Had that been an empty threat to alarm her? Or was it real?

Whichever it was, she'd better get back to camp and warn the others. They'd need to strengthen their defences. Because if Rex had been correct about the efficiency of the bulldozers, then what they'd done so far could prove far from adequate.

They worked all the next day to lengthen the barricades that ran immediately behind the hedgerows. They extended and widened the trench, even going as far as carefully sinking long, sharpened spikes of wood into the bottom. 'Hah!' snorted Zen. 'Let them try and get over that unscathed.'

By the time the sun was sinking beyond the horizon, they'd done all they could. It was up to Fate now.

Kristin trudged wearily back to her tent. She'd give all she possessed at that moment for a bath but, of course, that was impossible. She was just about to go into her tent and make do with a wash instead when something — a tingling at the back of her neck — had her swivelling around and staring towards the hedgerow that bordered the field. A figure was standing on the other side, head and shoulders hooded — perfectly still, just watching. Watching her? The memory of the other night returned with a slam, and she felt a stabbing of the fear she'd experienced then. This time, fortunately, she wasn't alone; she was surrounded by her friends.

Someone was trying to spook her; of that she now had no doubt. Well, they weren't going to succeed. In fact, she'd take matters into her own hands right now and put an end to their little game. She began to run towards the figure. It didn't move for a moment, but then, as if belatedly realising Kristin's intention, swung and swiftly vanished from sight.

Kristin increased her speed, but it was hopeless. The hedge was high and so dense that it hid the watcher's movements, so she couldn't see where he or she went, and by the time she'd reached the spot where she just about could look over it — just, there was no sign of anyone at all.

'Kristin,' Zen called. 'What's up?'

She sped back to him. 'Did you see anyone standing just there, on the other side of the hedge, watching me?'

'No, but then I wasn't looking. Who was it?'

'I don't know. I could only see the head and shoulders, and they were hooded. I couldn't even tell whether it was male or female.'

'Could it have been one of the Hunters? Sussing out what we, or you, were doing? The son seems very interested.'

Could it have been Daniel? No. She dismissed that theory almost instantly. The figure hadn't been tall enough. Or substantial enough. He could have got someone else to do his dirty work for him, though. Now and the other evening. Which would make his indignation over her insinuation positively hypocritical. And whatever Daniel was, she hadn't got him down as a hypocrite.

So, who could it be?

For the first time then, the name Rex popped into her head. Now there was a valid possibility. He wasn't particularly tall or well built. Could it have been him? Could they be acting in cahoots, trying to frighten her? Or, could Rex be taking matters into his own hands?

Because, as much as Daniel maddened and exasperated her, she simply couldn't see him being the type to deliberately scare her. Neither him nor his father. And his angry indignation in the wake of her impulsive accusation had seemed genuine.

Which led her back to the question — if she did indeed have a stalker, who the hell was it? And why would they be doing such a thing?

The hooded figure dashed along the lane, bending low so that nothing was visible above the dense foliage of the hedgerow. Kristin had moved much faster than expected. She'd looked scared. Good. That was exactly what had been intended. The tactics couldn't be allowed to fail.

It was time to up the game.

11

Two days went by and still there was no sign of any bulldozers. Had Daniel done a sneaky recce, Kristin wondered, and realised they'd have trouble getting any sort of machinery past the camp's defences? Or had his threat simply been an empty one, as she'd initially wondered, designed to propel the campaigners into some sort of mad panic? Forcing them to leave, even?

But if it had been merely scare tactics on the Hunters' part, the news — false or not — was spreading fast.

Richard showed up at the camp. 'Kristin,' he called as he walked towards her, 'have you heard the latest? The bulldozers are set to move in.'

'Yes,' she said, 'but Daniel threatened that two days ago and, as you see, nothing's happened. I think he was scaremongering.'

'Oh.' His expression lightened. 'Do you think so?'

She shrugged. She was nowhere near as confident of that as she made out.

'Um, actually, I came to ask . . . ' He hesitated, his expression now one of nervous uncertainty. Kristin braced herself for what she suspected was coming. 'Mum's been nagging me . . . '

'Oh?'

'That dinner she mentioned. Will you come — please? I'll get no peace till you do.' He grinned ruefully at her. 'No strings attached, I promise.' He tilted his head to one side, looking suddenly like a small boy again; an engaging small boy this time. He seemed able to change character at the drop of a hat. It was unsettling.

Kristin hardened her heart. Give his mother an inch, and Kristin guessed she'd be quickly grabbing the whole caboodle. And she wasn't going to give her the opportunity. She and Richard had to know that Kristin wasn't in the market for a serious relationship — and certainly not with a man who allowed himself to be so completely dominated by his mother. Goodness! Imagine her as a mother-in-law. It didn't bear thinking about. It was better to be open and aboveboard now, before Richard became even more attracted to her. What was it they said? 'Sometimes you have to be cruel to be kind.' Nonetheless, Kristin wanted to try and let him down gently. So she said, 'I can't, Richard; really, I can't. It's very kind of your mother, and I genuinely appreciate the offer, but-but I have to be honest — '

He didn't let her finish. His face had darkened as she spoke until it was just a fraction short of puce, all trace of the engaging boy gone. 'So that's a no then, is it?' His voice was harsh, his expression almost threatening.

Obviously her effort to be kind had failed. A smudge of alarm crept through her as she asked herself, what would such a man — a man able to transform himself so completely in a matter of seconds — be capable of? 'I'm afraid so,' she quietly said.

He sneered at her. 'It was just a dinner invitation, Kristin, not a marriage proposal. As I've already pointed out, there are no strings attached.'

'Does your mother know that, though, Richard?' Kristin risked saying. 'She does seem rather serious about things.'

'Things?' Richard spoke scornfully now. 'My mother simply wants to see me happy.'

'And I'm not the person to do that for you,' she haltingly told him. 'I'm not ready to settle down and that seems to be what she's planning for us.'

Despite her belief that it was best — for both of them — to be completely honest, she felt the worst she'd felt in a long, long time as she watched him walk away from her. Although it had to be said, that emotion was mixed with a feeling of deep-seated relief. Mainly because, for a split second, she'd glimpsed a darker side to him; a side that could possibly be capable of violence.

She watched him go. His shoulders had slumped and his head was down so low, his chin must have been resting on his chest. But she'd done the right thing. She was absolutely confident of that.

★   ★   ★

It wasn't long after that that she looked up from the book that she'd been reading to see Daniel's Range Rover parked in the gateway and him crossing the planks that someone had carelessly left in place over the trench. She saw him stop midway and look down, obviously at the spiked posts. He swung and began to walk across the field, his stride long and purposeful. He was heading directly for her. Even from where she was sitting, she could see the determined look to him. His mouth was compressed, his jaw chiselled granite. Oh Lord. Had he come to issue more threats? An ultimatum? Demand they remove the spikes, even?

But no. As he neared her, his expression softened until he looked almost genial. It was, once again, as if nothing of an argumentative nature had ever taken place between them. And she decided that if Richard was beginning to seem disturbingly mercurial, then Daniel was turning out every bit as unpredictable. Yet, he'd seen the spikes. Nervously, she waited for the harsh words, but all he did was smile and say, 'I've come to take you to Eve's for supper. My father's there.' He looked her up and down then, in that considering way that he had. The smile had vanished, leaving him looking almost critical. For heaven's sake, what was wrong with these men? They seemed able to change mood, if not colour, at a second's notice.

'You can have a bath,' he went on. 'I'm sure you'd appreciate that.'

She stiffened. Had he decided insulting her would be the best way forward? She wouldn't be at all surprised. 'Are you implying I'm dirty?'

'Not at all,' he smoothly replied. 'It's just that I can't imagine that the sanitary arrangements here are all they should be.'

She couldn't legitimately argue with that, so she didn't. She waited for him to go on.

'We thought . . . ' he said. 'Well, my father thought that we could have another go at discussing the best way forward, try and see if we can't accommodate each others' wishes and views. We're at a complete impasse as things stand at the moment.'

Kristin was rendered mute, such was her astonishment. That was what they'd tried to do that the other evening, but had got nowhere. So what would be the point of further discussion? Although, if Grant was there to act as some sort of referee — ?

He grinned. 'Well, that's a first. I've managed to silence you. Come on, Kristin,' he went on, 'it has to be worth a try, surely?'

'Kristin, everything okay?' It was Zen.

Kristin saw Daniel's expression change instantaneously. 'Why shouldn't everything be okay?'

'Mainly because we had some sort of weirdo peering over the hedge the other evening — um, two or three days ago, was it?' he asked Kristin. 'Whoever it was had a hood on, so she couldn't distinguish the face, or even whether it was male or female. But Kristin thought she was the target.'

Daniel swept his gaze back to Kristin. 'Is this true?'

She nodded. 'Whoever it was ran off the second I started to head over.'

His jaw tightened again, and his eyes darkened. 'In case you're wondering, it wasn't me.'

'I know. Too small in stature for you. But — '

'And before you say it,' he ground the words out, 'I also haven't paid anyone to spy — tail — stalk — whatever you want to call it.'

Zen was beginning to look alarmed. 'What's this? Tailing, stalking? What's going on, Kristin?'

'I'll tell you another time.'

However, he continued to look anxious.

'It's okay,' she assured him. 'I'll be fine.' She turned to face Daniel as Zen left them.

'It might be best if you stay at your mother's,' he quietly said. 'Who knows what sort of loony might be hanging around? It's quite clear, from what happened here and in the lane the other night, that someone is targeting you, and until we find out who and why . . . ' He was frowning as if he were concerned for her safety.

Again, she found herself wondering if that was genuine or just an act. 'I'm not deserting my friends — no way. Especially not with what's happening. We can't be sure it's just me. It could be everyone here.'

'No, it's you.'

He seemed very sure of that, she

decided. Why? Her doubts about his part in it all resurfaced with a vengeance.

'And you can wipe that look off your face,' he grimly retorted. 'It's not me. I would never do such a thing; never.'

'Okay, if you say so. Zen,' she called, 'will you all be okay if I go out for a while?'

'I'm a big boy now, as are the others. I think we can survive one evening without you.' He gave a broad grin. 'Don't worry, if your stalker returns we'll soon deal with him. He'll find he's taken on more than he bargained for. You take care of yourself.' His glance slid uncertainly towards Daniel.

'I'll look after her,' he called back.

'You'd better,' was Zen's terse response to that assurance. Nonetheless, he did seem to relax as he watched her and Daniel negotiating the trench.

★   ★   ★

It didn't take long once Kristin and Daniel reached Eve's house for Kristin to have her bath and change into something a little more glamorous than her customary jeans and T-shirt. She discovered a long-forgotten dress buried amongst her other garments in her wardrobe. It had been her favourite once. She put it on, pleased that it still fitted — unlike the top and trousers she'd worn for Eve's dinner party that first evening. Maybe she'd lost the couple of pounds she'd thought she'd gained? She wouldn't be surprised; she was under so much stress — what with her ongoing battle with Daniel and the question of whether she had a stalker or not.

'That's better,' Eve said when she rejoined them all in the sitting room. Kristin regarded her mother. She still looked subdued. Kristin could kill Stella. She'd well and truly knocked Eve's confidence for six. She hoped she'd told Grant what had happened. She needed his reassurance — Or maybe she had told him and his response hadn't been what Eve had hoped for. Kristin's heart sank. She hated seeing her mother like this; deflated, lacking that recently acquired joie de vivre. She'd been so happy to have met someone. Now, clearly, it was spoilt.

But whatever had happened between the two of them, there was still no mention of the article in the *Gazette*. Kristin could only assume that none of them had read it.

'What would you like to drink, Kristin?' Grant asked. He seemed to naturally assume the role of host for the evening, so maybe there was hope yet that he and Eve would get things together permanently. A hope which felt . . . well, contradictory to Kristin, when she considered her determined opposition to his and Daniel's plans for the village.

'Oh, um — white wine, please.' She was struggling to disregard the expression that was currently glittering within Daniel's eyes. Just as she was trying even harder to deny that she'd finally, and only after a great deal of humming and hawing, dressed with him in mind. But whatever her reason, she looked good. The dress was the exact shade of her eyes, which was why she'd originally bought it, with a low neckline that made no concessions to the full curves of her breasts. It also had a gently flared skirt that clung in all the right places and ended just above her knees.

She sat, with her legs crossed, extremely conscious of Daniel's keen-eyed and boldly appreciative gaze. In fact, she was so conscious of it that a couple of times she made a futile attempt to pull the skirt down over her thighs. She'd forgotten just how much leg it revealed once she sat down. Daniel manfully hid his smile as he watched her struggle in vain. He eventually murmured, 'You look lovely.' Then spoilt it by adding, 'I almost didn't recognise you as the woman I drove here earlier.'

Grant took his seat by the side of Eve on the settee, taking her hand in his as he did so. Eve smiled up at him; he smiled back. But Kristin could see the uncertainty behind Eve's tremulous smile. She wondered whether Grant did. Her heart ached for her mother.

'Cheers,' Grant said as he took a large mouthful of his gin. 'Now, Kristin, Daniel and I have been giving everything a lot of thought and we've come up with a plan.'

Oh Lord, was all Kristin could think. Now what? Five houses instead of ten?

'Seeing as you've already told Daniel you want the field examined for artefacts, how about if we hire an archaeological team to have a good dig around? They could use metal detectors, whatever it takes, to thoroughly check it all out; every inch. Then, in the event that they come up with nothing — '

'What makes you think they'll come up with nothing?' Kristin chipped in.

'In the event that they find nothing, and expert advice has assured us they won't, you and your fellow protesters allow us to go ahead unimpeded. How does that sound, hmmm? Fair?'

'And if they do find something? It could take weeks to carry out a full dig — months, years, even. Will you agree to wait?'

'For a reasonable length of time, yes — depending on what they find and the historical value of it, obviously. But we are committed to building there, Kristin, if at all possible. We've been granted permission, and the council are fully behind us. They want this development — in fact, the sooner the better were their exact words as I recall. They're genuinely convinced there is nothing valuable to be found. They wouldn't agree to us going ahead if there were. Plus, there's no hard evidence that there was ever an actual battle fought there. So, unless something significant is found, and quickly . . .' He shrugged.

Kristin interrupted then. 'The historical society are convinced there was a battle.'

Again, he shrugged. 'Could it just be wishful thinking on their part? You know, some sort of claim to fame for the village. Put it on the tourist trail. There's bound to be some profit in that for them.'

'Okay,' she agreed reluctantly. It was true. But if they did uncover valuable artefacts, the campaigners' case would be won. The proof was in the digging, so to speak. 'As long as we can stay there in the field to oversee the work, make sure it's not hurried, that nothing's missed — or more importantly, destroyed.'

Grant began to look doubtful at that, but Daniel intervened — surprising both her and his father, judging by Grant's expression of astonishment. 'Yes, we agree. But nothing will be destroyed, you have my word on that.'

'Daniel,' Grant said, 'are you sure?'

'Yes.'

Kristin too eyed him with suspicion. He'd agreed to her demand a bit too readily. Why?

But despite her doubts, it all sounded aboveboard. So once they'd agreed terms, their conversation took on a more general tone. And they were soon discussing their favourite music, books, food.

Once again, Kristin was surprised. She and Daniel had a great deal in common. Their favourite food was lobster. Daniel laughed and said, 'I don't suppose you get much of that on a campsite. I'll have to take you out for a day. We'll drive to the coast and try and find some just for you.'

They discovered they both loved the music of Mozart and Wagner, as well as Simply Red and Dire Straits. Their favourite authors were John Grisham and P.D. James.

By the end of the evening Kristin found herself liking both of the Hunter men, and it all seemed to end far too soon.

'I'll take you back, Kristin,' Daniel told her and, to her dismay, Kristin felt her heartbeat accelerating at the mere notion of their being alone together.

Would he try to kiss her again? Take her in his arms? All of a sudden, she longed for that. For his touch, for the feel of him close. Maybe this time, she'd go along with it for a bit longer. Just to see how it felt.

★　★　★

They were halfway back to the field when Daniel, completely out of the blue, asked, 'So what gives with you and that chap — Zen, is it? He seems pretty protective of you; one might almost say possessive — which seems a little odd for someone whom you've described as no more than a friend.'

'Oh, that's just Zen.' She decided not to mention the fact that once or twice it had been a little more than just friends. 'He looks out for me.'

He slanted a narrowed glance at her. 'He also looks pretty keen on you.'

'Not Zen. He's very much a free spirit.'

Silence descended then, and all too soon for Kristin, the gateway to the field loomed up in front of them, along with a deep sense of disappointment. He hadn't made any attempt to stop in one of the three gateways that lay along the lane, to kiss her, and now they'd be in full view of everyone in the field. Why hadn't he? Did she have to infuriate him before he could bring himself to try and make love to her?

Just at that moment, his phone rang. 'Oh, excuse me,' he muttered, viewing the small screen, 'I'd better take this.' He put the phone to his ear and said, 'Sophie, hi.' He then proceeded to listen intently before saying, 'Yes, okay — tomorrow it is then. Okay. See you then. Bye.'

Kristin made no bones about having listened to his end of the conversation. 'So how is darling Sophie?' she drawled. 'Still bitching?'

Daniel's expression revealed nothing as he said, 'Her bark's much worse than her bite.'

'Well,' Kristin snapped, 'you should know.' She didn't know why she felt so angry — maybe because he hadn't made any move to kiss her, but had agreed to meet Sophie the next day. That notion angered her even more.

His mouth twisted, whether out of amusement or irritation at her comment she had no idea. 'Sophie and I — like you and Zen — are just good friends, as they say.'

'Right, yeah. Course you are. Are you sure Sophie knows that, though?'

He turned his head, his eyes gleaming at her through the darkness. 'I'm sure. Sophie and I have been friends for years.' He tilted his head backwards and viewed her from beneath lowered eyelids. 'You're not jealous, are you?' The gleam intensified.

'Me?' Kristin scoffed. 'Jealous? What of?'

'Me and Sophie.'

'Don't be ridiculous.' The last thing she wanted was for him to guess she'd wanted him to kiss her. 'I simply don't like her.'

'You don't know her.'

'I don't need to. I've met her sort before: over-indulged, snobbish, rich, probably — or at least her family is. Thinks the world and its inhabitants revolve around her.'

'My word,' Daniel murmured, 'you do have a large chip upon your shoulder.' And he made as if to wipe it off.

Kristin slapped his hand away. 'Don't. Well, that's it then. We've reached an agreement. When can we expect the archaeologists?'

'In the next day or two.'

'Right. I'll be seeing you then.'

'Kristin?'

'Yes?'

'I meant it about taking you on a lobster hunt.'

Kristin didn't reply. He could stick his lobster. In any case, Sophie, she was sure, would swiftly put a stop to it. She well and truly had her claws into

Daniel. That was becoming increasingly apparent. Despite his avowal that they were only friends.

Nevertheless, as she trudged through the darkness towards her tent, she was forced to confront her acute sense of disappointment; more than that, try to make sense of it.

Why hadn't he tried to kiss her was the one question that kept repeating itself. He'd been directing admiring glances her way all evening — or had that all been an act? Had his attempts to kiss her been nothing more than pretence too? As she'd wondered more than once now, had it all been nothing more meaningful than a cynical ploy to soften her up, to persuade her and her fellow campaigners to leave the field? But for that to succeed, she'd have to convince the others to do the same. Yes, but if he'd made her believe he was falling for her, mightn't she have done just that? And now that she'd agreed to his and his father's proposal, well, he didn't need to either kiss her or bestow admiring glances. God! How gullible she'd been, to the point of stupidity. She'd even dressed for him this evening. She glanced down over herself. He must have been quietly laughing at her all the time.

And she still didn't trust them over this plan of theirs. They could easily have convinced the archaeological team to somehow manage to hide anything they found. She wouldn't put it past them to actually destroy any discoveries. And then, the thing that she hadn't considered at all: she still had to tell the rest of the protesters what she'd agreed to, without first talking it over with them.

* * *

The person lurking in the shadows had watched Daniel dropping Kristin off. Luckily, she hadn't noticed the hooded figure pressed against the hedge. Daniel hadn't lingered, he'd swiftly driven off again, and Kristin had disappeared into her tent. She hadn't looked at all happy; her brow had been creased into a deep frown.

The rest of the protesters had retired for the night, and the camp site was deserted. Which meant it was possible to crawl, unseen, through a tiny gap in the hedgerow. It was a struggle, with thorns and small branches tearing at the fabric of the dark coat, but manageable. The protesters hadn't extended the barricade this far, which meant that access could be gained to the tents; Kristin's tent, in particular.

The figure moved slowly, soundlessly, across the expanse of grass, a small cardboard box tucked securely beneath one arm. There was no sound from within the tent, so Kristin must have wasted no time falling asleep.

The intruder leant down and, placing the box on the ground against the canvas side of the tent, opened the lid. With that done, the person crept away once more through the gap in the hedge and disappeared from sight.

It would have been rewarding to stay and listen to the screams, but not sensible. Discovery would ruin everything. The bitch deserved it — because nothing was going to plan; nothing at all.

12

Kristin awoke suddenly. Something had dropped onto her head. What was it?

She put up a hand to brush off it off. Her fingers touched something small. It moved. She cried out in alarm as she swiped it away. The trouble was it was so dark inside the tent that she couldn't see. She reached out for the torch that she kept handy by the side of her and switched it on. She swept its beam across the sleeping bag, over the ground, over the tarpaulin upon which the bag was laid, searching for whatever it was that had dropped off.

And then she saw it.

Her screams woke the entire camp. Zen was the first to reach her. 'What is it? What the hell's going on?'

She scrambled, literally on hands and knees, from the sleeping bag and crawled as fast as she could out of the tent. It was as if the devil himself were in there with her.

'Oh God,' she gasped, 'spiders — everywhere.' She stood up and launched herself at Zen. She began to shudder. 'I can't stand them. It's the one thing I can't bear near me.'

Zen began to chuckle. 'I don't believe this. You live out of doors and can't stand spiders. You've never said anything before.'

Angry that he thought her fear amusing, she thumped him hard on his arm. 'Stop it; stop laughing. I've never seen them in this number before. Where have they come from?'

'Haven't a clue.' He poked his head in through the open flap and looked around the tent then; properly looked. They were alone. Their fellow campaigners must have retreated to their own tents once they realised the only danger was from a horde of spiders. 'I have to say, I've never seen this many all together before either. There must be ten, twelve of the little blighters.'

His laughter had stopped as he watched them running round the tent, climbing the canvas sides, disappearing beneath and into the sleeping bag.

Kristin spotted that too. Her face blanched. 'Oh no. I'll never be able to sleep in that again — '

Zen placed a comforting arm around her shoulders. 'Yes, you will. A good shake will soon dislodge them. Let's have a look round. Maybe there's a nest of them somewhere.' Outside again, his glance sharpened. 'Hello, what's that there?' He pointed to the small box propped against the side of the tent. He strode over and picked it up. It was empty.

'What's the betting that this is where they came from? But who on earth would have done such a thing? They would have had to go to considerable trouble to catch them and then to bring them here.' He regarded Kristin thoughtfully then. 'You say a stranger has been hanging round the camp, watching you, tailing you?'

Kristin nodded, her face even whiter in view of this discovery. 'Yes.'

'Then you've definitely got yourself a stalker. Someone who is deliberately targeting you, trying to frighten you. The first question is, who? The second, why?' He hesitated, eyeing her pallor, before saying so softly she could barely hear him, 'And thirdly, to what lengths will they go?'

* * *

They were questions that echoed over and over within Kristin's head all day. Who could be doing this to her? And, as Zen had asked, why? It couldn't be either Daniel or his father, surely. What would be the point, when they'd reached an agreement that suited the three of them? She decided to tell Zen, there and then, what she'd consented to.

'Fine,' was all he said, 'which makes it seem unlikely that your persecutor is either of them. So, if not them, who the hell can it be? One of the villagers? They want us gone, to a man and woman, if the Hunters are to be believed. Maybe somebody is banking on this sort of trick driving us away?'

And that theory began to seem look plausible when that same evening a small band of people — some of whom Kristin recognised as local — turned up at the gateway. They proceeded to form a line in the lane, shouting and waving their own banner, which said, 'We want you out of our village. You're not welcome.'

It started off peacefully enough, but before too long a gang of youths joined in and immediately started to tear down the campaign banners, calling, 'See this — this is what we'll do to you if you don't clear off.' Stones began to be heaved as they all took up the chant, 'Go away. We don't want you here. Go away. Out-out-out.' The campaigners sought refuge in their tents and tree houses.

'I'm calling the police,' Zen finally

said. Things were threatening to turn really ugly. The stones that were being thrown were getting bigger; they'd obviously brought their ammunition with them. They were also landing ever closer to the tents. 'Someone's going to get hurt at this rate. But I think we have the answer to your spider problem. It was undoubtedly one of these hotheads. He could be your stalker.'

Two police officers duly turned up, their sirens blaring, which meant the crowd hurriedly dispersed. A young PC leapt the ditch and strode towards the protesters. As an opening salvo, he said, 'Health and safety might have something to say about that trench and those spikes.'

Kristin heard Zen mutter, 'And we should care? Why?'

'Anyone hurt?' the PC went on to ask, as if that were the least of their problems.

'Fortunately, no.' Zen replied.

'Right. Well, you lot are very unpopular around here.'

'No,' Zen sarcastically riposted. 'We'd never have guessed, would we, Kristin?'

Kristin nudged him. There was no point in upsetting the police. They might need them at some time.

The PC stared long and hard at Zen and then went on, 'Well, they've gone now, but any more trouble — phone us.'

*　*　*

The next morning the team of archaeologists arrived — well, if you could call three of them a team. Zen and Kristin went to greet them.

'Where do you want to start?' Zen asked. 'I'll lay the planks down for you to get in.'

Within minutes, it seemed, they had organised themselves and begun work. Kristin and Zen watched their progress carefully. By the end of the first day nothing, apart from a couple of broken bottles, had been found. But then again, only a very small part of the field had been examined.

'This could take months,' Zen whispered to Kristin. 'Good tactics on your part to agree.'

'Yeah, I'm starting to see that.'

But that night it wasn't spiders that disrupted Kristin's sleep; it was thunder and torrential rain.

It was the rain that initially woke her, the sheer volume that was descending and drumming on the canvas roof of the tent. That and the steadily expanding puddle in which she was lying: it had submerged the tarpaulin and was now soaking her sleeping bag.

Once again, she scrambled out of it. Water dripped steadily through the tent, landing on her head as several claps of thunder seemed to reverberate right through her. Forked lightning lit up the interior of the tent as she became aware of the sounds of people running. She heard them shouting to each other, their voices rising as panic took over.

'Kristin,' Zen said, 'get out of that

tent. There's a deluge of water heading your way.'

She poked her head out between the tent flaps and saw what looked like a fast-flowing channel of mud, water and debris heading straight for her. Her tent had been pitched in a natural dip in the field, and the rain, falling so torrentially after several weeks of drought onto parched, hard ground, couldn't be absorbed quickly enough and so was forming a small river and was taking the most direct route down. To the spot where she was camped.

'Move — ' Zen's tone was an urgent one. ' — before you and your tent are washed away.'

Another even louder clap of thunder sounded immediately overhead as lightning forked viciously around them, illuminating the entire field. The rain was falling now with unbelievable force, forming a curtain through which she could barely see. Kristin did as Zen ordered and ran, aware of everyone dashing around, trying to salvage as much as they could. She looked back and saw her own tent collapse into a heap.

'Oh no,' she cried. All of her things — clothes, books, shoes — were inside. She turned and started to paddle through the muddy water towards it, but Zen held her back.

'Come on,' he shouted through the roar of rain and thunder. 'Let's try and find some shelter.'

'Where?' she shouted back. She spotted Elaine running towards them, followed by Shrimp and a few of the others.

'I think we need to get out of this field,' Shrimp said. 'Come on.'

They ran then, en masse, as successive flashes of lightning showed the water that was cascading everywhere, meticulously seeking out the dips and hollows in the meadow, many of them actually being formed by the movement of the water. It was washing away the work that the archaeologists had done that day. They'd be back to square one.

There was also the danger that if there were any remains waiting to be found, they'd be damaged beyond salvation.

There was a crack of thunder at the exact moment that lightning forked yet again — or that was the way it sounded. Kristin saw it hit the tree that she was passing but couldn't move fast enough to get out of the way. She screamed in terror as a branch split off from the main trunk, bringing a shower of foliage and twigs down with it. She felt a thump on her back and, in the next second, was pinned beneath it. She lay, stunned, hurting, her face pressed down into a patch of mud; water that, luckily, was running around her rather than over her.

'Kristin,' Zen yelled through the roaring of the storm, 'are you okay? Don't move. Don't move a muscle. Shrimp, Dave,' he called, 'over here — quick as you can. It's Kristin — she's down.'

Carefully, very carefully, the three of them lifted the branch off her. It hadn't needed Zen's bidding — she didn't move; couldn't move. The mud was sucking her down. She could barely breathe. It was in her mouth, up her nose —

Zen's tone was one of sheer panic now. 'Are you hurt? Oh my God.'

'I — I don't know. My back hurts,' she managed to moan weakly.

'Someone call an ambulance — now.'

'N-no.' Kristin had finally found the strength and fortitude to move. Everything seemed to work, miraculously — her legs, her arms. Somehow, the full weight of the broken branch seemed to have been held off her. 'Look — I can move.' Tentatively she lifted both her arms out of the mud. 'I'm fine.'

She struggled to turn over and then sit up. It wasn't easy, and it hurt agonisingly. But mercifully, nothing felt broken — badly bruised maybe, but not broken.

Headlights raked the night sky, slicing through the rain and lighting up the entire field. Zen stood up and started to run towards the beams, frantically waving his arms and shouting, 'Help! we need help!'

A man climbed from the vehicle and strode through the mud and fast-flowing water towards them. 'What's happened? Where's Kristin?'

It was Daniel.

13

Kristin had never been so glad to hear anyone's voice in the whole of her life. Daniel would take charge; she would be safe now. Which was a bizarre notion, considering that their every encounter ended in a fierce argument of some sort.

Daniel didn't seem to notice the devastation that lay all around. He only had eyes for Kristin, sitting in the mud, head propped in her hands, still dazed by what had happened. He made straight for her, his long legs negotiating the quagmire with enviable ease.

'What happened? Tell me.'

'I-I . . . ' she haltingly began. 'A branch broke off from the tree and flattened me, literally.' She gave a shaky laugh which almost at once changed into a deep-throated sob.

Daniel, disregarding the mud in

which she was sitting, knelt down by the side of her. 'Where does it hurt?'

'My back, but I think it's just bruised from the branch landing across me.'

He glanced up at Zen. 'Have you called an ambulance?'

'I was about to but Kristin assured me she didn't need it.'

Daniel returned his gaze to her. 'Can you move everything?'

'Yes. Look, if you help me, I'll stand — really. I'm positive I'm okay.' And once more, she moved both her arms and legs.

'Okay,' he reluctantly agreed.

With him and Zen supporting her by the arms, she did indeed stand shakily; at least she was upright. She blinked and tried to wipe the mud from her face, but she didn't think she was very successful. She suspected that all she'd done was smear it over an even larger portion of herself. Looking down then, she saw that water was literally dripping from every part of her. She gasped. Whatever must she look like?

'See? I'm fine. I'll just be a bit sore.'

Daniel looked around at the devastation all around them. 'Well, bruised or not, one thing's for sure — you can't stay here.'

Mercifully, the rain was easing and the storm sounded as if it was finally passing over. The flood water was already starting to drain away, apart from around Kristin's tent, where a small lake stubbornly remained.

'I'll take you back to Eve's — if the rest of you can manage till morning.' His glance skimmed over the crowd that had gathered around him and Kristin. 'I'll get help here then, to start putting things right. New tents, et cetera.'

Kristin and Zen stared at him in astonishment. Kristin had been sure he'd use this to suggest they all moved on.

'That's very good of you, mate,' Zen managed to say.

Daniel didn't reply to this. Instead he asked, 'Can you walk to the car, Kristin?'

'I think so, but I can't go to my mother's at this hour. She'll have a heart attack.'

'No, maybe not.' He was studying her thoughtfully. 'Okay. You'd better come back to mine.'

'Y-yours? What? Your apartment?'

'Yes.' He looked directly at her then, his expression a quizzical one. 'Is that a problem? I have some spare rooms so you don't need to worry about your reputation being compromised.' This was said in a slightly ironical tone.

'Oh — I wasn't.' She immediately felt ashamed of her suspicion over his motives for this display of generosity. He was being so kind. 'It's just . . . well, I wouldn't want to put you to any trouble. It is practically the middle of the night, after all.'

'You won't,' he briskly assured her. 'It'll be my housekeeper who'll have the trouble.' There was a definite twinkle to his eye now.

She couldn't help herself; she grinned back. She watched as the harsh planes of his face softened, then heard a snort from behind her and realised that Zen was still standing there — the only one who was. The rest of the group had dispersed to begin trying to salvage something from the wreckage. He was visibly struggling to suppress his laughter.

'You go, Kristin,' he urged. 'You need to rest that back. We'll manage here. Start to put what we can right. Just look after her, mate,' he then told Daniel.

'Oh, you can be sure I'll do that,' Daniel replied, a strange expression now crossing his good-looking features.

Kristin narrowed her eyes at him once more with suspicion. However, his guileless stare revealed nothing of whatever his thoughts might be.

★   ★   ★

With support from both men once again, she managed to negotiate the rain-drenched grass and then the planks across the trench to the gateway.

Shafts of pain were shooting up her back and she found herself wondering if she'd been premature in her belief that she hadn't damaged anything. But eventually, they did make it to the Range Rover and Daniel lifted her up to gently place her in the front passenger seat.

'Thank you,' she murmured gratefully.

'My pleasure,' he softly said, the silvery gleam of his eyes perfectly discernible through the inky darkness. 'Comfortable?'

'Um — yes.' Although she wasn't; her back really hurt.

'I'll get the doctor to have a look at you when I've got you back to the manor.'

'Will he come at this time of the night?'

'For me he will.'

She softly snorted. Of course he would. Why would she have thought otherwise?

★ ★ ★

It took only minutes to reach the gates of Woodcote Hall. Daniel opened them using a remote control and then left them open once they'd passed through. For the doctor, Kristin presumed. The actual house stood at the end of a winding driveway. She'd never been close enough to see it properly before, screened as it was from the roadway by dense thickets of trees and bushes.

She stared at it. My God, it was huge. It stood, three floors high — Georgian, she thought, though she wasn't very knowledgeable about period houses — and built from what looked like red bricks, although being dark she couldn't be sure of that. It had row upon row of windows; so many, in fact, she quickly lost count. A steeply sloping grey slate roof topped the impressive building and supported a legion of ornamental chimney pots.

Daniel pulled to a halt on the circular driveway immediately in front of the entrance — an entrance that boasted a truly magnificent portico — before striding round to assist Kristin from the vehicle. Very, very gingerly, she climbed out.

The rain had practically stopped by this time and miraculously the moon was making tentative appearances, as it played hide and seek with the remaining clouds. At least her fellow protesters would have some light to help them begin clearing up. She'd felt bad about leaving them, but what choice had she had? She'd have been no use to them, injured as she was.

'Okay?' he asked.

'Yes, just about. What a gorgeous house,' she then said.

'I like it.'

'It's huge — even just the ground floor.'

'Yes. So there's more than enough room for the occasional visitor.' He slanted a knowing glance at her.

Something occurred to her then. Did Sophie live with him? This seemed a very palatial apartment for just one person.

'Um — does Sophie live here too?'

He studied her for a moment, his head cocked to one side, before saying, 'No.' And, judging by the abruptness of that single word, that was all he intended to say on the subject.

He helped her up a couple of shallow steps and through the front door. This led into a black and white tiled hallway large enough to contain the better part of her mother's ground floor. A flight of stairs led off this, up to the other apartments presumably. He then opened another door straight into a second hallway, almost as large as the first one. This was where his accommodation began, presumably.

The floor here was also tiled and had several pieces of what looked like genuine antiques positioned against the walls. There was a high-backed, ancient-looking wooden settle; three equally old ladder-backed wooden chairs; an oak chest; and, central to all of this, a circular pedestal table upon which sat the biggest bowl of perfumed roses she'd ever seen. The walls were wood-panelled and hung with oil paintings, one of which could have been a Monet, but probably wasn't. Even Daniel wouldn't have that much money, surely?

One question had been bothering her all through the drive here. 'Um — why did you come to the camp tonight?'

'I was still up, reading, and so I heard the storm raging. I could see it was right over the campsite, so I thought I'd just check you were all right.'

She darted a frowning glance at him. That almost sounded as if he cared about her. His response to her glance was instantaneous. Clearly, he'd interpreted her expression for what it was: scepticism. Again, she felt ashamed of herself.

'Kristin, we might disagree about the development, but I wouldn't want to see you — any of you — hurt in any way.' His words were harshly spoken, but she had no doubt that he meant them.

It must have been the direct result of

all that had happened; the sheer stress of everything — her terror as the lightning struck and the branch fell, her aching back, or maybe the fact that yet again she'd angered Daniel — she didn't know which had been the trigger. But in the next minute she gave a small sob, and almost involuntarily she covered her face with both hands and began to quietly weep.

'Kristin, please don't . . . '

'S-sorry, I-I can't help it.'

'Oh, God.'

She heard his groan. He sounded as if he were in as much pain as she was, and sensed him moving towards her. He gently pulled her hands away from her face, and then she was in his arms, her face pressed to his chest, as she sobbed out her fright, her pain — her emotion.

'S-sorry,' she again said. 'I can't help . . . It's silly, I know.'

'No, no; it's the shock of it all,' he soothed, beginning to rock her gently from side to side. 'It's a perfectly natural reaction.'

'Ouch,' she gasped.

'Oh God, sorry. I wasn't thinking. That must hurt.'

Her sobbing intensified. 'It does — any movement does.'

'Ssh, I won't do anything to hurt you, I promise,' he murmured, holding her even closer. He kissed the top of her head. She looked up at him, her eyes tear-drenched, luminous, framed by lashes that looked like wet silk. She watched as his own eyes darkened, moistened; and then all thought fled as he lowered his head and laid claim to her lips.

His kiss was one of hunger and passion, and Kristin couldn't stop herself. She kissed him back, clutching at the front of his jacket and moaning softly in the back of her throat. This was what she wanted; needed. He pulled her even closer, his hands gentle on her back, following its natural curves, cupping, stroking, caressing, as he parted her lips and began to drink thirstily of the sweetness he found within. She was helpless beneath her need of him. It was as if this had always been meant. As if they were meant . . .

But then he was pushing her away from him, putting a space of several inches between them. She felt bereft; lost. 'Sorry,' he muttered. 'I didn't intend for that to happen. I'll call the doctor.' He walked swiftly to the telephone sitting on a side table, his expression such that it was as if he had never held her; never kissed her.

Kristin stared at his back, stunned into silence. What had happened? Something that had so repelled him that he thrust her away from him, undeniably rejecting her.

Oh no — please, no. Did she stink; was that it? Surreptitiously, she lifted an arm and sniffed at herself. She was wet through but she didn't smell.

It must have been something else. Had she been too eager? Was that it? And what about Sophie? He was involved with her. Had he belatedly remembered Sophie?

A sensation of deep dejection, mixed with the most extreme anguish, swept through her. No, no, no! The truth hit her in a dizzying, headlong rush.

She'd fallen in love with him — deeply and irrevocably.

She closed her eyes and gave a low groan. How stupid could she be? Daniel Hunter was so far out of her reach, he might as well be on another planet. Jupiter, say.

She heard him talking to the doctor. 'Okay. If you could come. I'd really like her checked over. She is in a great deal of pain. Thanks.'

He replaced the receiver. 'Right.' There was a remote, shuttered look to him now. A look that seemed to warn, 'Don't get too close.'

'He's coming straight over. Come on, let's make you comfortable in here.' He led the way into a room just off the hallway. It was a small sitting room with invitingly deep cushioned settees and armchairs.

'Daniel?' It was a woman's voice. Both he and Kristin swung — Kristin very, very gingerly. Every movement, even the smallest, was beginning to hurt more and more. Despite her caution, the movement still made her wince. She saw a small woman standing in the doorway.

'Oh, Jane,' Daniel said. 'This is Kristin Lacey.'

It could have been the middle of the day instead of the middle of the night, Kristin decided, so matter-of-fact was his tone.

'Ah, yes, I've heard all about you.' The woman walked into the room smiling, with her one hand out-stretched. There was no indication of any kind of anger over Kristin's part in the protest against the man who was her employer. And yet her loyalties must lie with him, surely? 'My good-ness, what's happened to you?' Her concerned glance took in Kristin's soaked state.

'Storm damage. Kristin, this is Jane,

my housekeeper.'

'Hello.' Goodness knew what the woman must be thinking. 'It's very nice to meet you.' She chewed at her bottom lip. For heaven's sake, couldn't she come up with something a little more original under the circumstances? Which weren't exactly commonplace.

'I've brought Kristin back here because she's hurt her back.'

'Oh, dear me.' Jane frowned in concern. 'Would you like me to call Doctor — '

'I've already done it, thank you. But perhaps you could prepare a bedroom. The pink one, I think. Would you mind?'

'Of course not.' And she very evidently didn't. Which made Kristin wonder what sort of wage Daniel paid her to make her so willing to get up in the middle of the night and start making a bed. 'Actually, the pink room is already prepared. I like to keep a couple of bedrooms ready in case of an emergency, and this is certainly an emergency.'

261

Kristin couldn't stop herself from wondering whether Sophie ever stayed in the pink room. Or, as was much more likely, did she share the master bedroom? The stabbing pain that that notion induced outdid every other agony that she was experiencing and was further proof of her growing feelings for Daniel.

'Would you like to go to your room, Miss Lacey?' Jane gently asked.

Kristin looked at Daniel, searching for some sort of clue as to what she should do.

'It's okay, Kristin, if you'd rather do that.'

'I would, yes,' she agreed. 'I'd like to lie down.'

'Okay. Jane, would you do the honours, then?'

'Of course. Please follow me, Kristin — Is it okay if I call you that?'

'Yes, please. Thank you.'

★ ★ ★

The pink bedroom, when they got there, was an absolute dream. It made Kristin's room at Eve's look like a broom cupboard in comparison. It was the last word in luxury and good taste. Pink was a bit of a misnomer. The only pink item in the room was the carpet, and that was such a delicate shade it looked almost cream. The king-size bed had a lemon, ivory and green canopy over it, and its pale green duvet was heaped with an abundance of pastel-coloured silk cushions. The walls were ivory, as were the generously sized wardrobe and vanity unit. There was a chaise longue covered in the same fabric as the canopy, as well as a couple of armchairs, again in ivory. In front of these was a flat-screen television which, she imagined from its position, could also be viewed from the bed. There were a CD player and a radio, both of which could be operated from the bed if needed. A large book case against one of the walls contained a comprehensive selection of books. There was no chance of her getting bored, that was for sure.

'Will this be all right for you?' Jane asked.

'I'll say so. I've been more accustomed to pretty basic accommodation — namely, a tent.'

Jane laughed. 'Oh, I see.'

Kristin heard the sound of a doorbell.

'That'll be the doctor,' Jane told her. 'I'll go and let him in and then bring him up to you. You get undressed.' She went to a drawer in the vanity unit and pulled out a fine cotton nightshirt which she laid on the bed. Did they keep spare nightwear, Kristin wondered, for unexpected guests? From this evidence they apparently did. 'And hop into bed. Oh — ' An anxious frown creased her brow. ' — will you need some help?'

'No, I'm sure I'll manage. I-I just need a towel.'

Jane indicated a door. Kristin hadn't noticed it until then. 'En-suite through there. You'll find towels and everything else you might need.'

Kristin, due to having very speedily washed off the remnants of mud that had been still clinging to her, had only just managed to crawl beneath the duvet when the door opened and Jane ushered in a tall middle-aged man.

'This is Doctor Patterson, Kristin. I'll leave you now, Doctor.' She left the room, quietly closing the door behind her.

'Right — Ms Lacey, isn't it?'

'Yes. Thank you for coming, but really, it could have waited until the morning.'

'Oh no. Mr Hunter — Daniel — was most insistent, and one doesn't say no to him — as I'm sure you're aware.' He gave her a twinkling smile. 'It's no trouble. Now, would you like to turn over on to your front and lift your nightshirt? Daniel told me it's your back.'

'Yes.' Kristin slowly and carefully did as he asked, thereby revealing the part of her back that was troubling her.

'Oh, yes, I see. The bruise is already coming out. Now, tell me if this hurts.'

After one of the most comprehensive examinations she'd ever been subjected to, Doctor Patterson covered her again and said, 'You'll be pleased to know that I think — no, I'm positive — it's merely bruised. All I can recommend is rest for a couple of days. You can get out of bed, of course, but don't go running around.'

Kristin snorted with amusement. 'That's the last thing I feel like doing. In fact, I doubt if I could.'

'I would recommend that you stay here.'

'Stay here?'

'Yes. It's out of the question for you to return to the campsite — for a while, at least.

If I were you, I'd have a hot bath and take some painkillers. They should help you to sleep.'

'Um, my mother lives in Huntleigh.'

'In a house?'

'Yes.' Kristin was puzzled. 'It's only

me that likes a tent.'

The doctor smiled. 'No, what I meant was it might be easier — less painful — to avoid stairs for a day or two.'

'Oh yes, I see.'

'You'll be very stiff for a while, I would imagine. You've had a heck of a knock there. You're very lucky no serious damage was done.'

Once he'd left again, there was a tap on her door. Thinking it was Jane, she readily called, 'Come in.'

It was Daniel.

She tugged the duvet up over her, but not before she saw the gleam in his eyes as his gaze skimmed over her. The fabric of her nightshirt was very fine and she was only too conscious of the way it outlined her body.

'The doctor thinks it would be advisable for you to stay here, so . . . '

'Yes, he said. Are you sure that will be okay?' She peered anxiously up at him.

The intriguing little gleam that she

was becoming so familiar with appeared in his eyes. 'Perfectly. I wouldn't hear of you staying anywhere else. It will be my . . . pleasure.' His voice was so smooth it made her think of chocolate; dark, rich chocolate.

His pleasure? Now what exactly did he mean by that? And how on God's earth, in her weakened condition, was she going to be able to hide her feelings for him if she had to spend any length of time in his company, just the two of them? That was the most pressing question of all.

14

By mid-morning of the following day, the camp had been more or less restored to order. Daniel had sent along some new tents to replace the storm-damaged ones, as well as sleeping bags and fresh supplies of food. The protesters had worked tirelessly erecting the new tents and managing to salvage some, at least, of their belongings. Kristin's tent had been completely destroyed, as had most of her belongings.

Zen was re-hanging the banners which had been torn down for a second time in the ferocity of the storm when Richard turned up. 'I thought I'd come along and see how you fared through the storm.' He looked around. 'Are those new tents?'

'Uh-huh,' Zen said. 'Daniel Hunter sent them.'

'Dan — ' He looked astonished and not too pleased, truth to tell. 'Where's Kristin? I can't see her.'

'No, she was hurt last night. A branch broke away from that tree.' Zen pointed towards the object in question. 'It dropped onto her, sending her flying into the mud and hurting her back.'

'No. Oh my God. Where is she? In hospital?'

'I'm not absolutely sure. I wouldn't think so; she'd have let me know. Daniel turned up out of the blue, and he's taken her back to his place. I'll give her a ring if you like — oh, no, I don't think she'll have her mobile phone with her. It must have been in her tent — and that was destroyed.'

'Oh my goodness. Mum will be most anxious to know about this. She's grown very fond of Kristin. I'll try and get her on Hunter's number. I need to know that she's okay. Oh dear me, what a catastrophe. Poor, poor Kristin.' And with that, he hastened away again.

* ★ ★ ★

As for Kristin, after luxuriating in a deliciously hot and scented bath, she did manage to finally get some sleep. Mainly because the bed she was in was the most comfortable she'd ever lain in. It was as if it were tenderly moulding her body, supporting and comforting it; and this, along with the painkillers that she'd taken, ensured a deep, dreamless slumber.

She was awoken by Jane carrying in a tray.

'I've brought you some breakfast. You must be famished after your ordeal last night.'

She set the tray down on the bed. It had leg supports that unfolded to make a small table. Kristin struggled to sit up. She couldn't suppress her groan of pain. Her back, if anything, was hurting even more this morning, and that was accentuated by her stiffness.

'Oh dear, back no better then?' Jane asked, concerned by the spasm of anguish that passed across her face.

'Not really, no. But Doctor Patterson warned me I'd be stiff.' She grimaced. 'He wasn't wrong about that.'

'I'll bring you some more painkillers.' Jane went to the window and drew back the floor-length curtains to allow the morning sun to shine in.

It was hard to believe that they'd suffered such a violent storm the night before. The sky was an unbroken blue and the birds were rejoicing in that fact by singing their little hearts out.

Jane opened the window. 'There, some lovely fresh air. That'll make you feel better.' She then swivelled to look searchingly at Kristin. 'You've got a bit more colour this morning.'

'This is very kind of you.' She indicated the tray of food. There was a bowl of what looked like cornflakes covered in milk, a croissant, a glass of orange juice and a small pot of coffee. 'I don't want to be any trouble.'

'You won't be. I like having someone else to look after. It makes a change from just one man. Now — ' She was suddenly brisk. ' — Daniel asked me to tell you that he's had to go out. An appointment he simply couldn't rearrange.' Sophie? Kristin couldn't help wondering. 'He'll be back by late afternoon. You're to rest and recuperate; he was most insistent about that. Also, he said you're to make yourself completely at home. And he asks if you will eat with him — seven o'clock, in the dining room. Is that all right? Will you be up to it?'

'Oh, yes.' Kristin was taken aback. 'No — I mean, yes, I'm sure I'll be up to it.' What was the matter with her? She was stammering and stuttering like the worst of idiots. And all because Daniel had asked her to have dinner with him. It wasn't as if it was the first time, after all. But then again, it was the first time in the privacy of his own home. Was that why she was so nervous?

'Right. Well, I'll leave you to eat your breakfast in peace. If you should need me for anything, anything at all, just press number one on the phone.' She pointed to the phone on the bedside table. 'That goes directly through to the kitchen. And please, feel free to ring anyone you want. Your family and friends must be worried about you.'

'Thank you, that's most kind.'

After hungrily consuming every morsel of her breakfast, she climbed from the bed very, very gingerly and limped into the en-suite bathroom. She ran herself another hot bath, this time adding some of the expensive-looking bath oil that sat on a shelf. The oil, combined with the hot water, acted like a balm on her bruising. She sighed with pleasure as she lay back and soaked.

Once she was dressed, she carefully made her way to the window. Her room was at the rear of the apartment and looked out onto a picture-postcard view of immaculately kept gardens. A man — the gardener, she presumed — was dead-heading an enormous bed of roses. She pushed the window wider, allowing the morning warmth to flood in. The perfume of the flowers reached her; a heady, fragrant scent. She took a deep breath and watched a bumble bee gorging itself on a nearby honeysuckle, after which it flew, somewhat drunkenly, past her. She smiled to herself. Heaven must look like this. The gardener glanced up and seeing her, said, 'Good morning.'

'The garden looks wonderful.'

'Thank you.' And he bent to his work once more.

She decided she'd better ring her mother before Eve heard about her accident from someone else. She just hoped she wouldn't fuss.

It took several rings of the bell at the other end of the line before Eve answered. 'Mum,' Kristin said.

'Oh, hello, darling,' Eve said. 'I was just about to ring you.'

'Don't bother. I'm not at the camp and I've probably lost my phone.'

'Well, where are you then?'

'I'm — um, I'm at Daniel's.'

'Daniel's?' Eve's astonishment echoed down the phone line. 'What on earth are you doing there?'

'The camp was all but washed away last night in the storm. And a tree branch broke off and landed on me.'

She went on to relate the events of the night, but Eve sounded faint, distant — as if she had other things on her mind. She did ask, 'Are you all right?'

'A bit bruised and sore, but that's all. Mum, are you okay?'

There was a pause lasting for several seconds. Then, 'No, not really. Stella's still making trouble. She keeps ringing me, telling me to leave Grant alone.' Eve's voice broke and then quivered. 'In fact, I thought you might be her again. She's certainly persistent.'

'Have you told Grant about this?' Kristin indignantly demanded.

'Yes. I also told him what she told me about his affairs.'

'What did he say?'

There was a short pause and then

Eve said, 'He admitted to one affair — just one and a very brief one. He said Stella had been so cold, so unfeeling towards him, always complaining no matter what he did. He was so desperately unhappy that he turned to someone else. He'd suspected that she'd had several affairs, but he stayed with her for Daniel's sake. In the end she left him and, well, you know the rest.'

'Yes. So what's he going to do?'

'Have a word with her; tell her he's not going back to her. He-he begged me not to leave him.'

'There! That's good, isn't it?'

'Is it? He's used to glamorous women, thin women, which there's no denying I'm not.'

'Oh, Mum, you're lovely.'

'I-I told him I'd be here for as long as he wants me — which might not be very long. Stella rang me a little while ago and said he'd just spoken to her, and he is thinking of going back to her but doesn't want to upset me — which,' she added with a shaky laugh, 'I have to say sounds just like Grant.'

*　*　*

Kristin lay on the chaise longue, a cushion in the small of her back in an attempt to ease the persistent and deep-seated ache that even painkillers couldn't seem to remove entirely. She'd put down the book she was reading and was staring out of the window, turning over in her mind all that Eve had told her, when the phone rang. Luckily, it was of the cordless variety so she had taken the precaution of placing it on a table by the side of her.

She picked it up with a feeling almost of dread. What if it was Eve again, to tell her that Grant had ended things?

But it wasn't. It was Richard. Jane must have put him straight through. Daniel had obviously installed a very sophisticated state-of-the-art phone system throughout the apartment. But then, looking at all the evidence around her, he could easily afford it.

'Kristin, I've just heard what's happened. I'm so anxious about you. Are you badly hurt?'

'No, no, just bruised, but it's kind of you to ring.'

'Look, I've had a chat with my mother and she suggests that you come to us, rather than be cooped up with Daniel Hunter. I'll come straight over and fetch you — just say the word. Only if you want to, of course. It would be no trouble.'

'Well, that's very thoughtful of you and your mother, but . . . ' She could hear Iris in the background.

'Oh, let me speak to her, Richard, for goodness sake. Of course she must come.'

There was a muffled exchange and then Iris was on the line. 'Kristin, I'm so concerned about you. You can't possibly stay with that man. He'll grab the opportunity, with you so helpless, to press the case for his wretched development. We can't have that. In your weakened state, there's a risk you'll agree to anything he suggests. Now, I insist you come here. You can have a complete rest; I'll nurse you, cook for you. Richard is beside himself with worry.'

Kristin grimaced. Richard hadn't sounded beside himself. He'd sounded quite calm, as a matter of fact. 'As I said to Richard — ' she began.

Iris broke in. 'I refuse to take no for an answer.'

'No, really, Mrs Millard — '

'Iris, please. We're friends, aren't we?

'Well, yes, but I'm really not up to going anywhere. I can hardly move, never mind tolerate another car journey. And as you know, my mother's nearby. I can go to her as soon as I feel up to it.' Not that she wanted to do that. Eve had quite enough on her plate without having an injured daughter thrust onto her as well.

'Tssk, you won't want to worry your mother. Richard will be most careful. He'll bring my car. It's more comfortable than his; more room.'

Kristin took a deep breath. 'No,

thank you for your offer, but I'm fine here — really.'

'But you're in that man's house. Utterly at his mercy. Who knows what he'll do?'

'Daniel has been kindness itself.'

'Huh! I bet he has.' Iris snorted derisively. 'I've heard all about him and his-his various women. I know his sort. I should do. Richard's father was just the same. Only cared about himself, could manipulate for England when it was something he wanted.'

'Mother!' she heard Richard exclaim.

'Mrs Millard ... ' Kristin firmly emphasized the title. The last thing she wanted was any sort of intimacy with this unpleasant, dictatorial woman. And why on earth would she go to Richard's house when her own mother lived in the village? 'Within a couple of days I'll be returning to the camp. Until then, I'm staying here. Thank you for your concern. Goodbye.'

Exasperated beyond measure, she stabbed at the off button. Poor Richard.

He must be hard pressed to get a word in when Iris got started. But for goodness sake, he was a grown man. Why didn't he get his own place, his own life?

★ ★ ★

Kristin remained in her room, relaxing and recuperating, as she'd been instructed to do. It was no hardship, not with so much luxury surrounding her. It was also the perfect opportunity to catch up on some reading and listen to some music. The choice of both reading matter and music was comprehensive. Eventually she had settled on a Ruth Rendell novel as her choice of book, and for music, Mozart.

It was almost six o'clock before she heard the sound of the front door opening and then closing. She listened intently. The firm stride across the tiled hallway indicated that Daniel had returned from wherever he had spent the day. She heard the low murmur of his voice as he spoke to Jane, and then a knock sounded on her door. Her heartbeat quickened as her pulse rate simultaneously raced. She prayed she'd be able to conceal her growing feelings for him.

'It's me, Daniel.'

She grinned to herself. Who else would it be, for heaven's sake? It was his apartment.

'Come in, please.' Her voice shook. She laid the book down on the table and using the remote control, lowered the volume of the music. The door opened and Daniel strode in.

'How are you feeling?'

'Not too bad.'

'You're still a little pale.' He stood over her, his narrowed glance inspecting every inch of her. Her nerve endings tingled; her breath caught in her throat. It had felt as if he were physically touching her. 'Back still hurting?'

'A bit. But I think it has improved slightly.'

'Do you feel up to coming out for

dinner? Sorry — ' He grinned unexpectedly. ' — that makes it sound as if you're under lock and key. Do you feel like joining me for dinner, is what I should have asked.'

She smiled. 'Well, it hasn't felt as if I've been under lock and key. I've enjoyed every second. I can't recall the last time I simply lounged around all day. But yes, I'd like to join you for dinner. If you're sure, that is?' Belatedly, she wondered if he'd rearranged other plans to stay with her. Plans with Sophie, maybe?

'I am.' His gaze rested on cheeks that had suddenly flushed pink. 'That's better. A few roses.' He put out his hand to touch her cheek. His fingers lingered, the tips gently moving over her skin, turning the gesture into a caress. It was the only way she could think of to describe it. But whatever it was, it was all she could do not to nestle her cheek into his palm.

As it was, her entire body tingled as her skin burned beneath his touch. Had he meant to make her feel that way? Or had it simply been the sort of sympathetic gesture he'd make to anyone who'd been hurt?

When he took his hand away, Kristin felt oddly abandoned.

'Okay, well, I'll go and change then.'

'Oh.' Did that mean he dressed for dinner? She had nothing to change into. Jane had laundered and pressed the jeans and T-shirt that she was wearing, but other than that . . .

Her expression must have registered her dismay because he said, 'You're fine as you are, but you'll need a change of clothes to take you through the remainder of your stay. I'll see to it.'

What on earth did he mean, he'd see to it? Did he keep an assortment of women's clothes, as well as nightgowns, here at the apartment? And when he said the remainder of her stay, how long was he planning to keep her here? Was she, in fact, a prisoner — even though she wasn't being kept under lock and key?

15

She spent the next hour carefully considering these questions, uncertain what to make of it all. What to make of Daniel, come to that. Once again she'd set her book to one side, quite unable to concentrate on it. At this rate she was never going to finish it. The trouble was, the deeply disturbing memory of Daniel's fingers gently caressing her cheek kept getting in the way of the words. Could it be that he was every bit as attracted to her as she was to him? He had kissed her, after all. And it hadn't been any ordinary kiss; it had been urgent, demanding . . . passionate.

It took another knock on her door to bring her out of her reveries about Daniel. It was Jane. 'Okay if I come in?' she asked.

Kristin realised it must be nearly seven o'clock. 'Of course.'

Jane walked into the room. 'Daniel asked me to give you these.' She was holding several bags, all of them with the name of a well-known and expensive department store on them. 'They've just been delivered. You'll have time to change if you want to.'

Kristin took them from her and peered inside. There were T-shirts, a couple of pairs of jeans, two dresses, a lightweight sweater, toiletries, cosmetics — in short everything she could possibly need for a short stay. There were even some undies. She could make out lace, silk — had he selected them? Her cheeks flamed at the mere thought.

'I took the liberty of guessing your size. Twelve, right?'

Kristin nodded, dumbstruck. 'How on earth did he get hold of all these? He must be a miracle worker.'

'Oh, you obviously don't know Daniel very well. Once he makes up his mind to do something, things happen very quickly.'

'I'll say. But surely the shop would

have been closed?'

'No, late opening. Daniel's been a very good customer of theirs for several years. So when he phones, they bend over backwards to accommodate him, even putting on a delivery service for him. Now, are you ready for dinner?' Jane asked. 'Or I can wait if you want to change.'

'Do you know, I think I will change. But I can make my own way along. You needn't wait.'

'Are you sure? You're still looking a bit stiff.'

'I'll be fine.'

'Okay. Well, Daniel's in the small sitting room, that's the third door on your left. Go along when you're ready.'

* * *

It didn't take Kristin long, despite her stiffness, to strip off her current outfit and change into one of the dresses. Daniel had obviously taken note of the kind of thing she liked because, once on, it looked perfect. It was also an excellent fit, thanks to Jane. The dress was the colour of her eyes, a rich violet blue, and had a scooped neckline, a close-fitting bodice and a gently flaring skirt that reached to her knees. At the bottom of one of the bags she found a pair of wedge sandals that matched the dress almost exactly. Everything that she pulled out looked expensive and beautifully made. How was she going to pay for it all? The items looked as if they'd cost a lot more than she would normally pay for anything.

Even the cosmetics were of the very best quality. She quickly applied some and at once felt better. She viewed herself in the mirror. Her eyes still looked strained but the dark shadows that had been traced beneath them had gone. 'Hmmm, not bad, considering.'

So that was it; she had no more reason to delay joining Daniel in the sitting room, and it was already fifteen minutes past seven. She left her own room and made her way along the corridor. It still hurt to move, but not quite as badly as it had the night before. Maybe the regular doses of painkillers were finally paying off.

Daniel was waiting for her, just as Jane had said he would be. He stood up as she walked in and moved to her side.

'Thank you,' were her first words, 'I don't know how you managed this,' she said, indicating the dress, 'but it's all perfect.'

'Oh, I called in a favour or two. It all fits then?' She nodded. 'You can thank Jane for that. I wouldn't have had a clue.' He cocked his head and grinned boyishly at her. 'You look lovely.'

'Thank you, but you'll have to let me pay you for them.'

'I wouldn't hear of it. Regard it all as a present.' He walked with her to the nearest armchair and gently eased her down into it. 'Comfortable?'

'Yes, thank you. You have a truly lovely home.' She gazed around the room. She knew she'd been in it the previous night, but nothing had really registered that well. Now she saw that it was a moderately sized room, almost cosy, in fact, furnished once again luxuriously with a thick carpet, comfortable furniture, a state-of-the-art music system, a couple of side tables, lamps . . . She wondered if he'd had everything professionally done, or was it all his own taste? Somehow she couldn't imagine a man as strong-minded as he was submitting to someone else's selection of furniture and decor for his home.

He shrugged as if it was of no consequence. 'I like it. I've opened a bottle of champagne. Would you like a glass before dinner?'

'I'd love one, but I've just taken some painkillers, so . . . ' She frowned. She didn't have a very good head for alcohol at the best of times. It only took a couple of glasses of wine to have her head spinning.

'Just one glass shouldn't hurt. In fact, it might even do you good; ease the pain a little.' He poured a modest amount into a crystal flute and handed it to her. Their fingers brushed and Kristin felt her heart leap. Daniel didn't seem to notice the fleeting contact. He lifted his glass and said, 'Here's to your recovery.' A smile flirted with the corners of his mouth, even as his eyes gleamed at her, and he softly said, 'But not too quickly.'

This time it wasn't just her heart that leapt in her breast at his final words. Her entire body began to tremble; even her breath caught in her throat. What did he mean, not too quickly? That he liked having her here? He didn't want her to leave? She took a steadying gulp of her champagne. It didn't help.

He returned to his own chair and sat down again, his gaze not leaving her for a second. Kristin cast around wildly for something to say and came up with precisely nothing. In desperation she stuttered, 'Um . . . th-the archaeological team turned up.'

'Oh, did they? How did they get on?'

'Slowly. Unproductively.'

'That should please you all.' This was drily said. 'Despite the fact that they're finding nothing. After all, the longer it takes, the more time will pass before we can begin work — and the better the chance of them eventually finding something.' Silvery eyes glinted at her over the rim of his wine glass.

Kristin wasn't sure how to take that. Was he being sarcastic? She decided to allow him the benefit of the doubt and ignore his words. 'I think the storm will have undone most of what they've achieved, if not all of it. There was water and mud everywhere.'

'Yes, I saw.' His mouth tightened. 'You were very lucky not to have sustained more severe injuries. The weight of that branch must have been considerable. Has no one told you that it's dangerous to stand under trees during a thunderstorm?

'I wasn't standing under it,' she retaliated. 'I was merely passing beneath it. We were trying to get out of the field.' He said nothing in response to that so she went on, in an attempt to lighten the sudden tension that had arisen between them. For it had sounded as if he was blaming her for her accident. 'I wonder how they've got on with the clearing up?'

However, he gave no further indication of it if that was indeed what he was doing, because all he said was, 'I called in on my way back here. The tents had arrived and the food. It all looked more or less back to normal. Oh, that reminds me. Zen found your phone and, amazingly, its charger. Lord knows how, but they both still seem to be working.' He stood up and went to one of the side tables. 'Here they are.' He handed them to her.

'You've been very kind, Daniel. Thank you.'

'I might disagree with what you're doing,' he murmured, 'but, as I said before, the last thing I want is for anyone to be hurt.'

With that, the door opened and Jane said, 'Dinner's ready.'

The meal was delicious: smoked salmon and prawns to start, then fillet steak delicately coated in a gorgeous red wine and shallot sauce with the largest selection of vegetables that Kristin had ever seen. They finished with an apple and blackcurrant tart served with thick clotted cream.

She sat back and, placing her hands over her bloated stomach, quietly moaned. 'Wow! That's added several pounds to my weight, I'm sure.'

Daniel threw his head back and laughed. 'You're not seriously telling me that you have to watch your figure. It's perfect.' He took a mouthful of his wine and watched her over the rim of his glass.

'Thank you,' Kristin said, astonished. 'But I can assure you I do have to watch it.'

'A pleasure that most men, me included, would willingly undertake on your behalf.' His gaze didn't leave her, not for a second.

Kristin felt the heat of a blush creeping up her face; her pulses raced almost out of control. She'd never felt like this before; like a teenager. Well, at least not since she actually was a teenager. How did he manage to do what no one else could?

He then proceeded to add to her discomfort by chuckling and saying, 'I do love a woman who blushes. It's a rare treat these days, sadly.'

Which must have been what made her ask, 'Doesn't Sophie blush?' She gnawed at her bottom lip. Where had that come from? She hadn't meant to mention the other woman.

'I'm sure she must do at times.' His tone was impassive now, so impassive it could have been a different man talking. Even his eyes had cooled, although he was still staring at her. 'As I said once before, Sophie and I are just good friends.'

'Just good friends?' Her tone implied she didn't believe him.

Daniel's face hardened as he ground out the single word, 'Yes.'

'So who do you see on more than just a friendly basis?' She couldn't believe she'd just asked him that. What on earth was wrong with her? She glared accusingly at her glass of red wine. She knew she shouldn't have had it. Although Daniel had been quite correct; it had eased the aches and pains.

He cocked his head to one side. 'You mean, who am I dating?' She nodded. 'No one at the moment — although I'm hoping that will soon change.'

What the blazes did that mean? That he had his sights set on someone? Who? She only just stopped herself from asking him that too, but that might be a step too far. In any case, she didn't really want to know, and she doubted that she'd know her. She didn't exactly mix in Daniel's set. 'Do you know,' she said instead, 'I think I'll go to my room. I'm really, really tired.'

If he was disappointed at this abrupt ending to the evening, he gave no indication of it. All he said was, 'I'm not surprised, after the events of last night. You couldn't have got much sleep.'

'Well, not as much as I'm used to, certainly.' She got to her feet, preparing to leave the table.

Daniel also stood up. 'I'll take you to your room, to make sure you get there.'

'Where else would I go?' she blurted. 'Or are you worried about your precious possessions? I might be an eco-campaigner, but I'm not a thief.'

Fury, dark and menacing, blazed at her then. 'I'll pretend you didn't say that,' he ground out.

Again, Kristin couldn't believe what she'd said. What was happening to her? Her tongue seemed to have developed a will of its own. 'I-I'm sorry. That was unforgivable.' How could she be so ungrateful — rude, even — after he'd been so kind? If only the floor would open up and swallow her, she'd thankfully disappear. It didn't, of course. That would be too simple. Instead she was left standing, the object of his searing gaze.

'Yes, it was,' he grimly agreed. Nonetheless, he proffered an arm for her to hang on to. 'I would hardly have brought you here if I'd thought that of you.'

They walked back to her bedroom in silence, Daniel considerately matching his longer stride to her shorter, slower one. They reached the door and she quickly let go of his arm — too quickly; she staggered without the support he'd been providing.

He grabbed hold of her again almost at once, steadying her. His one arm slid around her waist as he roughly pulled her against him. She winced. He ignored it. His head came down and his mouth captured hers. There'd been no hesitation, no uncertainty. He knew what he wanted and he was ruthlessly taking it.

16

The kiss literally took Kristin's breath away. Her head began to spin as Daniel ground his lips savagely over hers. It was as if he were punishing her for her words of a moment ago.

Then, as she was surrendering totally to him, he released her, reaching beyond her to open her door, and all but pushed her inside. 'Goodnight, Kristin. Sleep well.' And without another word he had gone.

Kristin stared after him, lifting fingers that trembled to lips that felt swollen and bruised. What had that been about? Punishment? Yet it hadn't felt like punishment; his passion had been all too evident.

She walked into the bedroom and across to the mirror, where she regarded herself. She looked like a woman who'd been thoroughly made love to. Her lips were indeed swollen, her eyes wide and luminous. She was in love — head over heels, helplessly in love with Daniel, the man she was so committed to fighting against. There was no denying it. So when had dislike — she wouldn't call it hate, it had never been that, even during their most heated arguments — turned into love? She didn't know. It had crept up on her, conquering her resistance; conquering her.

She'd just climbed into bed, her eyes heavy and dull with fatigue, when her mobile phone rang. She picked it up and responded. It wasn't anyone she knew because no name appeared on the small screen.

'Yes?' she replied.

No one answered; there was only an echoing silence.

'Who is this?'

The sound of heavy breathing was all she could hear. A crank call. She switched the phone off. But then something occurred to her. Could it be her stalker? But how would he have her number? Unless it was someone she knew — someone she'd given her number to.

It rang again. She pressed it against her ear. 'I don't know who this is, but please stop.'

A muffled, distorted voice spoke. It was unrecognisable, as if someone were talking through some sort of barrier. 'You should remember who your friends are. Daniel Hunter only wants one thing — to build his houses. He doesn't care about anything else; not our heritage, not you.'

'Who is this?' she burst out.

But the phone went dead. Whoever it had been had ended the call.

Kristin stared at it, her expression fearful. Who could be doing these things to her? Not Daniel; he wouldn't be warning her against himself. Or would he?

Her eyes widened. Could he be playing some sort of weird game with her? But why? Her heart lurched in her chest. And if it was him, then here she was, completely at his mercy in his house. Injured, defenceless. Was that the sort of man she'd fallen in love with? Manipulative, cruel, coldly calculating?

★ ★ ★

The following morning she had a visitor: her mother. Jane showed her into Kristin's bedroom. Kristin was reclining on the chaise longue in front of the window, watching the gardener at work.

'Darling, how are you?' Eve cried. 'I've been so worried. Grant said I should come and see you, satisfy myself that you're still in one piece.'

Kristin got to her feet. 'Well as you can see, I am.' She hugged her mother.

'This is so good of Daniel,' Eve said, 'considering.'

'Yes. How's Grant?' She didn't really want to get onto the subject of Daniel. She might be tempted to admit her love for him and, for the moment, she wanted to keep that to herself. Mainly because Eve might tell Grant, and Grant might tell Daniel. And that was the very last thing she wanted.

Eve, luckily, accepted the abrupt change of subject and shrugged. 'Fine . . . you know.'

'And Stella? Is she still bothering you?'

'No.' She eyed Kristin. 'Has Daniel mentioned her?'

'No, not a word, but then why would he?'

'No, I suppose he wouldn't.' Her expression was one of curiosity, tinged with what looked perilously like hope. 'But I was wondering, have you changed your mind about him? I mean, you are staying in his house.'

'Not really, no.'

'Does Daniel know that?'

'Yes.'

Eve looked disapproving. 'Rather ungrateful, wouldn't you say?'

'Who is?' She knew very well who her

mother meant, of course.

'You.'

'I didn't ask to come here. He simply brought me.'

★   ★   ★

However, her mother's words did make her even more determined to return to the camp. She didn't want to get too accustomed to this way of living. It could make her extremely loath to return to a tent. She'd leave in the morning.

She ate alone in her room that evening. Jane had told her that Daniel had gone out. Business, she'd said. Huh! More likely avoiding her, Kristin decided. That notion thoroughly depressed her, despite her ongoing suspicions of him.

To distract herself from these reflections, she rang Lizzie. Lizzie would cheer her up. She always did. But this time, her friend failed her.

'How can you stay at Daniel's house

when you so mistrust him?' she indignantly cried. 'Isn't it a bit hypo-critical?'

Kristin didn't bother arguing with her. Lizzie and her mother were absolutely right. She was being hypo-critical and ungrateful. The sooner she left Woodcote Hall, the better.

She did just that the next morning, bright and early. No one was about, so she could slip out without risking seeing Daniel and having him try to persuade her to stay. Not that she thought he would. He'd most likely be glad to be rid of her. In fact, he was probably regretting bringing her here; that and their kiss.

She called a taxi. Luckily for her, the gates weren't closed, so she could wait on the roadside. Within ten minutes she was being greeted with cheers and smiles by her fellow campaigners.

'How are you?' Zen asked. 'Are you sure you're fit to return?' He regarded her with concern.

'I'm fine. Bit sore still, but nothing

that won't pass.'

'And what did his lordship think of you leaving?'

'If you mean Daniel, he doesn't know.'

'He doesn't know?' he echoed. 'You mean you sneaked out of the house?' She nodded. 'Bit rude, wasn't it, after all he's done?'

Kristin slanted a glance at him. He'd changed his tune. He was actually sticking up for Daniel. 'He'd have tried to stop me.'

'Well, there was no rush about you returning. Richard's been keeping an eye on us. Did he ring you? I told him you'd got your phone back. He asked for your number. I hope I did right, but I gave it to him.'

Kristin's heart did a somersault. Could her malicious caller have been Richard? In fact she wondered, and not for the first time, could he be her mysterious stalker? He — and his mother — were both getting very possessive of her.

307

But why would he do such a thing? They were on the same side. She supposed it could be some convoluted form of rebellion against his mother's domination. He was powerless to stand up to her, so he decided he'd exert some sort of authority — control, even — over Kristin. But it still didn't really make sense. He liked her; more than liked, she increasingly suspected. Could this be his way of getting closer to her? She frowned. How would scaring her out of her wits achieve that?

She sighed. She was tired of it all, in truth. Against all expectation, she'd felt safe at Daniel's, despite her recurring doubts about him possibly being her stalker. She'd thought long and hard about that and had eventually concluded that it couldn't be him. She refused to believe she could be stupid enough to fall for a man capable of terrorising a woman. While she'd been at the manor it had felt as if nothing and no one could reach her; harm her. Here at the camp she felt vulnerable again. Maybe she shouldn't have come back; should have waited a bit longer.

Oh, to blazes with it all. She'd hang on for the archaeological team to come up with its conclusions and then, whatever those conclusions were, she'd call it a day. She'd get herself a job, a flat, a proper life once again. She'd more than done her bit for the environment. Let someone else take up the cudgels.

With that decided, she crawled into her tent and slid inside her sleeping bag. Within minutes, she was asleep.

★ ★ ★

She was awoken in what felt like only seconds afterwards by Zen calling her. 'Someone here to see you, Kristin.'

Her heart quite literally leapt. Daniel? Had he discovered her disappearance and come to make sure she was all right? A painful stabbing of guilt made itself felt. Zen was right; she had been rude. He and Jane had both been so kind, and that was how she'd thanked them. She had left a note on top of the neatly folded pile of clothes that he'd bought for her. She hadn't felt she could keep them — not even as a gift, as he'd suggested. But now, in retrospect, she could see that the note hadn't been thanks enough. In fact, she'd been downright ungracious. Eve would be appalled. She'd always insisted that good manners must be exhibited at all times.

Groaning, she scrambled to her feet; she was still more than a little shaky, it had to be said. In no fit state to be confronted by a possibly angry Daniel. And, as if that wasn't enough, her back was aching badly once more.

Mustering her courage, she parted the tent flaps and went outside to see not Daniel standing there, but Sophie. Despite her misgivings over possibly having to deal with Daniel's fury, her heart nevertheless sank at the fact that it wasn't him.

But what on earth was Sophie doing here alone? It could only be for one reason. She'd heard about Kristin's stay at the hall.

'Can I help you?'

Zen had walked away, leaving the two women to whatever it was they had to discuss.

'Yes,' Sophie hissed, leaning towards her, so close that Kristin could feel the warmth of her breath upon the skin of her face. 'You can stay away from Daniel for starters.'

'Stay away,' Kristin snorted. 'He practically kidnapped me.'

'Oh, really?' It was now Sophie's turn to snort contemptuously. 'I've heard of some pretty over-the-top ways of grabbing a man's attention, but standing under a tree in a storm takes the prize.'

'Surely you don't think I did that deliberately?' Kristin couldn't hide her shock.

'Well, didn't you?'

'Why would I risk injury — even death? I didn't know the branch would break off. Just as I didn't know Daniel would turn up at that precise moment.'

For the first time, Sophie looked unsure of herself. 'Daniel is a very kind, caring man. You really didn't expect him to check on things here?' Her scepticism came through, loud and clear.

'No, I didn't. The thought didn't occur to me. It was the middle of the night.'

'Yes, well, just stay away from him. I mean — ' She gave another snort — of amusement this time. ' — staying at the hall. You must have realised what an imposition that would be.'

'That wasn't the way Daniel saw it, clearly. Otherwise he wouldn't have insisted I remain. He'd have taken me to the hospital and left me there.' Sophie again looked unsure of her ground. 'How did you know I'd been there, anyway?'

'I called in to see Daniel about . . . It's none of your damned business,' Sophie belatedly cried. Kristin shrugged nonchalantly. 'Anyway,' Sophie went on, 'just

stay away from him. He loves me and-
and you're just an embarrassment to
him. He's as good as said so. We're
practically engaged, if you must know.'

'Oh, only practically?' Was this really
her talking? So coolly, so calmly? When
her heart felt as if it were being literally
torn apart — with all the pain and
anguish that that entailed.

'And what does that mean?' Sophie
glared at her.

'Nothing. It doesn't matter a jot to
me how engaged you are, practically or
fully.'

'So, if you've got any ideas about you
and him . . . '

Kristin gave a shout of laughter. How
was she doing this — staying so in
control of her shattered emotions?
'Ideas? Why would I have ideas about
him? In case you hadn't noticed, we
play for opposing teams.'

'Yes, well, just keep it that way, do
you hear me?'

'Oh, loud and clear. Goodbye,
Sonya.'

'It's Sophie,' the other woman practically shrieked.

★ ★ ★

Once Sophie had gone, Kristin retreated into her tent, to sit on the ground — well, on her sleeping bag — with elbows on raised knees and her head in her hands as she turned everything over and over in her head, trying to make sense of it. Who was lying here, Sophie or Daniel? Daniel had assured her that he and she were just friends. But Sophie was insisting they were practically engaged.

Anger, raw and searing, suffused her then. *Oh, get over it*, she told herself. Had she really believed she and Daniel would get together? She snorted at her own naivety. A fox and a hen had more chance of making a go of it.

No. As she'd previously decided, it was time to get on with her life. Time to leave Huntleigh for fresh climes. Leave Daniel to Sophie. She was much more his type. She had to accept that she'd been deluding herself, thinking that he might have feelings for an eco-protester other than those of exasperation at her obstinacy. He'd never made any secret of those sentiments. But then, how did she explain those passionate kisses?

She was still trying to work out what his game was when, for the second time, she heard Zen call, 'Another visitor, Kristin. You're very popular all of a sudden.'

'Oh Lord, who now? Once again she stood up. She felt like a jack-in-the box: up, down, up again. If it was Richard come to pester her about having dinner with him and Iris, he'd get short shrift. In fact, she might well ask him outright if he was her stalker. She was well and truly fed up with it all.

But it wasn't Richard who strode into her tent, it was Daniel; a Daniel, moreover, who was exhibiting every sign of being absolutely furious with her, just as she'd feared.

17

'What the hell is this?' he demanded, shaking what she could see was her note at her.

'It looks like the note I left you.'

'So is that it?' He unfolded the piece of paper and read, with withering contempt, 'Need to get back. Thank you for all you've done. Kristin.' He then crumpled it up in his fist before throwing it on to the ground. Rage flashed from his eyes.

'Well, I did need to — '

'I'm so glad you appreciated all I've done.' He deliberately and exaggeratedly stressed the last three words.

'I did, but I thought I might be outstaying my welcome. I . . . ' She was about to say she'd thought he was avoiding her, when he forestalled her.

'Oh, and you also left these.' She hadn't noticed him putting the bags onto the ground. He lifted them up now and all but heaved them across the tent. They landed on her sleeping bag. His gaze fastened onto it as if he'd only just noticed it. 'Don't tell me — that's where you sleep?'

She looked at the heaped-up sleeping bag, viewing it through his eyes. 'Yes.'

'For God's sake.'

'What's wrong with it?' What a stupid question. She could see perfectly well what was wrong with it.

'Well, if you can't see that for yourself, I'll tell you, shall I?' He paused and then when she didn't speak, went on, 'You've injured your back — badly. How will lying on that heap help it?'

Once again, she had no answer for that. Because let's face it, she told herself, he did have a point.

'What? Speechless?' he cruelly mocked. 'Surely not.'

Anger, every bit the equal to his, made her lunge at him, her instinct to attack him. 'Don't-don't you — '

He caught her raised fists before they could land a punch on him, and roughly pulled her towards him. Pain shot through her — not that she was about to let Daniel know that. He'd only gloat that she'd proved him right.

Their faces were a mere inch apart as he slid an arm about her and ground out, 'Don't — what? Don't do this?' And he pressed her against him so hard their chests painfully collided. Kristin did wince then, after which all thought was extinguished as he bent his head and began to kiss her.

Kristin heard a low groan and realised it was her. Oh no. How was she going to have the strength of will to resist him? She didn't. Helpless against her own desires, she started to respond, parting her lips, allowing his tongue to explore, to taste her honeyed sweetness.

'Kristin . . . ' He deepened the kiss and his arms tightened around her, crushing her to him. 'I want you — so much. Please . . . '

And that was all it took; those three

simple words. I want you. Kristin felt as if cold water had been thrown over her. He wanted her. Not loved her; wanted her. Why? Because it was Sophie whom he loved? Maybe she should confront him — ask him why he was kissing her when he was practically engaged to another woman? But then, he might think she cared.

She dragged herself from his arms. 'No — stop.'

But he didn't seem to hear her. He tried to pull her close again. His eyes were half-closed so it was impossible to read their expression. She did what she had to do to save her sanity. She lifted both hands and pushed him away. 'No.'

His eyes snapped open with that and he stared at her. 'Why not? You want me to — '

'No, I don't.'

'Huh! You could have fooled me then.' His lips were tightly compressed now as he stared at her, his expression grim; unyielding. 'Tell me, do you respond to other men like you do to me? Practically inviting them to make love to you?' His top lip literally curled. He couldn't have made his scorn, his contempt for her more obvious. He despised her.

'How dare you?' she spat. 'I would never invite anyone to make love to me. And certainly not you.'

He gave a harsh laugh. 'No, stupid of me to think such a thing. You wouldn't need to, would you? Here you are, surrounded by men; you can take your pick.'

'That's right,' she mendaciously assured him. 'I can. And as for you — well . . . ' She too now snorted her disdain. 'You have the lovely Sophie. So why on earth are you bothering with me?'

He didn't take his eyes off her as he bit out, 'Yes, why am I bothering? Okay, have it your way. Go on living in this-this — ' He waved a hand in the air, indicating the tent, the camp. ' — slum.'

'It's not a slum!' she shouted.

He raised an eyebrow at her. 'Have

you looked around lately? It's a slum. A dump. There's rubbish everywhere. Clothes hanging all over the place, pots and pans left everywhere and anywhere. In my book, that's a slum.'

'Get out; just leave. I never, ever want to see you again.'

'I can't grant that particular desire, I'm afraid,' he drawled. 'You'll be seeing a great deal of me. Particularly when I come to evict you all from this field — which shouldn't be too much longer now, I would imagine — in the complete absence of any sort of discovery, valuable or otherwise. But till then, I'll bid you goodbye.' He swung and strode from the tent and, she suspected, although he had denied it, from her life.

Once he'd gone, she slumped down onto her so-called bed and covered her face with her hands. The tears flowed — literally a deluge, and completely unstoppable. She loved him with all her heart, and he . . . well, he only wanted her. No mention had been made of loving her, and she refused to settle for anything less.

* * *

Either Zen heard her weeping, or somehow he sensed her distress, because he came to sit down with her. He put an arm about her shoulders and pulled her close. 'Is this because of him? Daniel? What did he do — say?'

She dashed away her tears and shook her head. 'It's my own fault entirely.'

'Why's that then? Because you love him?'

She gazed at him, her eyes wide and dark. 'Oh God, is it that obvious?'

'Uh-huh. Well, at least it is to me.'

She covered her face with both hands, the tears spilling over yet again.

'Actually, what I came to tell you is . . . ' He regarded her reflectively. 'Well, it's more bad news, I'm afraid.'

Oh no. Now what? How much more could she take?

'They're — the archaeologists, that is

322

— convinced that there are no treasures to be found. The bowls that were initially uncovered have no historical significance at all. In their opinion, this was never a battlefield. They can't see much point in continuing. Looks like the Hunters will get their way.'

It wasn't too much of a surprise to Kristin. She'd already begun to suspect as much.

'Look,' Zen went on, 'you're in no fit state to remain in a tent. Why don't you go home to your mum's? We're going to pack up and move on. I think you've had it with this way of life, haven't you?'

Kristin nodded, her heart too full for a moment to speak. Zen had always had this ability to read her thoughts before she spoke them. 'Sorry.'

'Don't be. You've more than done your bit.'

★ ★ ★

So that was what Kristin did. It only took her a matter of minutes to pack her belongings. She had very few left, after all, apart from the things that Daniel had bought her. So, after saying goodbye to everyone, she returned to Eve's. Eve, she knew, would be pleased to hear she'd given up the life she'd been leading for the past nine months. All Kristin had to do now was decide what she was going to do in the future.

She let herself into the house, dropping her bags onto the floor. She was about to call out when she heard voices — her mother's and Grant's. She could hear what Grant was saying quite distinctly.

'I love you, Eve; not Stella. I don't care what she's been saying. She knows damn well I stopped caring about her years ago. She's just a vindictive woman lashing out, trying to spoil things for us.'

Kristin was smiling to herself as she heard Eve murmur, 'Oh, Grant, I love you too.'

'So marry me. There's nothing and no one to stop us.'

'Only Kristin,' she heard Eve groan. 'Lord knows what she'll say.'

Kristin strode into the kitchen. 'Kristin will say go for it. And congratulations!' And she put both arms around her mother.

Eve looked positively shocked. 'B-but what about the field? It will make things a bit difficult between you and Grant, not to mention Daniel.'

'You don't have to worry about any of that that. The protest is over. The others are moving on. We've been assured the meadow was never a battlefield; there's nothing to find — to protect.'

Eve's face fell at that. 'So you'll be moving on too?'

'Not straight away. In any case, I'm done with all of that. I'm going to get a job, settle down.'

'Oh, darling, I'm so pleased.'

'Well,' said Grant with a smile, his delight plain to see, 'I think that calls for some champagne, don't you?'

★ ★ ★

The next afternoon, Kristin decided to walk back to the meadow to say a proper goodbye to all her friends. She hadn't done it the day before in the wake of her and Daniel's fierce row. All she'd been able to think about was returning home.

She was only part of the way there when she noticed the rain clouds building once more: dark, purple, intensely threatening. The drought was well and truly at an end. She should have worn a coat, was all she could think. All she had on was a lightweight shirt and a pair of cotton cut-off trousers, and they'd be soaked through in minutes. She quickened her pace, but not enough. Just as she'd feared, the rain began to fall and soaked her not within minutes, but within seconds.

With the first clap of thunder, and ignoring the pain in her back, she broke into a jog — which was why she didn't hear the sounds of a car coming up behind her.

'Kristin,' she heard someone call. She

swung and saw Iris Millard peering through a partly open window at her. 'If you don't mind sitting in the back, I can give you a lift.'

'Oh yes, please.' She could see the bag of shopping on the front passenger seat but she wasn't about to refuse the offer, as much as she disliked the woman. 'I'm on my way to the campsite.'

A gratified smile lifted the thin lips. Kristin felt a surge of guilt. Maybe she'd been a bit hard on her, consistently refusing to go for dinner. It wouldn't have killed her, she supposed.

'Jump in then,' Iris said. Kristin gratefully did so. Iris turned round to look at her. 'My goodness, you look soaked through. That won't do you any good, not after your accident.'

'No, I know. I just hope I don't spoil your car upholstery.'

'It'll dry again.'

Iris pressed her foot hard onto the accelerator and the car shot forward.

To say Kristin was surprised would be something of an understatement. She hadn't got Iris down as a fast driver. She must have been watching too much *Top Gear*. She grinned briefly to herself as the car ploughed through the ever-deepening puddles, catapulting water high into the air behind them. But it wasn't long before the amusement gave way to darts of misgiving. Iris hadn't spoken since those initial words; which, considering the way she normally talked — practically non-stop — was strange. Unnerving, even.

Kristin eyed the back of the older woman's head. Something didn't feel right. Even so, it wasn't until she sighted the gateway to the field, and realised that Iris had no intention of stopping, that she spoke. 'You can drop me here.'

Iris ignored her, and it was then that she felt the first twinge of alarm — real alarm — especially when she heard a click. The older woman was leaning forward over the steering wheel, presumably to see through the heavy rain.

'Iris,' Kristin again said. They'd passed the gateway. 'Where are we going? You've passed the gate.'

'We're going home. To my home,' the older woman grimly said.

Kristin's initial sense of alarm intensified. She reached out a hand and tried the door handle nearest to her. As she'd already feared, childproof locks were activated. Incredibly, she seemed to be a prisoner. 'Iris, the door's locked. Could you — ?'

But it was as if she hadn't spoken, because Iris went on, 'Richard wants to speak to you. He has some sort of plan to stop the development of the field once and for all. We have to save it.'

'He doesn't need a plan. It wasn't a battlefield, it seems, and there's absolutely nothing buried there. Would you please unlock — ?'

But again, it was as if she hadn't said anything. Iris snorted. 'Is that what

Daniel Hunter told you? You shouldn't listen to him, Kristin, you really shouldn't. He's got his own agenda.' She swivelled her head to look at Kristin. Her eyes were blazing; beads of sweat freckled her brow. 'He's nothing but a liar. Listen to Richard.'

'It wasn't Daniel who told me. Iris, please — stop the car.' She could hear the panic in her voice now, but if Iris heard it, she didn't respond. She turned her gaze back to the road ahead, her shoulders still hunched over the steering wheel.

'Please stay quiet,' Iris said at length. 'I'm doing this for your own good.'

Real fear stabbed at Kristin then. What was going on here? Was she being abducted? No — Iris was an elderly woman. Why would she do such a thing? The notion was preposterous. 'Iris, please . . . Th-this could be construed as kidnapping.'

'That's right. You should have remembered who your real friends are.' The words were a low hiss. 'I tried to warn you on the phone. You've forced me to do this.'

Kristin's eyes widened as realisation finally struck. 'It's been you — scaring me, stalking me. All the time it's been you.'

18

'Yes, that's right. You were supposed to turn to Richard for help, for protection, not Daniel Hunter. Never him. Whatever were you thinking of? Well, you're going to do the right thing now. I'm going to see to that.'

Kristin was speechless. The woman must be insane. There was no other explanation. 'Iris, please. You can't just-'

Iris swivelled her head and stared at Kristin once more. Her eyes were so dark they were almost black, their pupils enlarged to practically fill the eye. For the first time in all of this, Kristin wondered if she was on some sort of drug; if that was what was making her behave in such a weird way.

'Just what?'

'I've already said — kidnap me.'

'Why shouldn't I? You have to be

made to see sense if you can't see it for yourself. It's for your own good. Richard is devoted to you. Why can't you see that? You're breaking his heart — just like his father broke mine. Well, I'm not allowing you to do that.'

'This is against the law. You can't . . . Please, please stop the car, now. It's not too late. I'll forget everything that's happened.'

'Oh no you won't. You've got to be helped to do the right thing. I won't have Richard hurt, I won't. He's all I have.'

Kristin again tried the door handle. It was still locked. She was trapped, at the mercy of this crazy woman. Nausea rose in her throat. 'I'm going to be sick.'

'No you aren't. We've arrived,' Iris breezily said, for all the world as if Kristin were just visiting for afternoon tea. They had stopped in front of a pair of cottages. 'Now then, don't make a fuss. There's no one to see in any case. The neighbours are out at work. I'm going to come round and open the door, and I want you to walk inside with me. Richard's in there.'

Quietly, wordlessly, that was exactly what Kristin did. Richard would help her, she was sure of that. She simply couldn't imagine him going along with his mother's crazy plan, any more than she wanted to. He couldn't have realised that his mother would actually kidnap Kristin, surely?

She'd already decided there was no point trying to run away. Her back was too painful and stiff which, as Daniel had furiously pointed out, was most probably due to lying on the sleeping bag and the hard ground upon which it rested. It wouldn't take much effort on Iris's part, despite her age, to catch her again. And how would she reach the village on foot, anyway? In her condition, it would take her hours. They must have travelled three or four miles at least.

She'd have to rely on Richard having more common sense than his mother, to understand that what she was doing was a crime. They walked side by side to the door, Iris's arm threaded through hers, as if they were the best of friends.

'I couldn't believe my luck,' Iris said chattily, 'when I saw you all alone like that. I couldn't let the opportunity pass, you see. You do understand?'

Iris opened the door and they walked into a small hallway. She then led her into another room directly off this and switched on a light. At first glance Kristin assumed it was a cloakroom; there were coats hanging on pegs on a wall. A second glance revealed that it was nothing more than a cupboard; a large cupboard, but nonetheless only a cupboard.

'He's in here,' Iris said.

He wasn't, and before Kristin had time to react Iris had darted back out and closed the door behind her. To Kristin's horror, she heard the sound of a key turning in the lock. 'Iris,' she shouted, 'don't do this. Whatever will Richard say?'

There was no answer, although

Kristin could sense her presence still on the other side of the door.

'You can't keep me here.'

'Yes I can. Until you agree to take Richard seriously. Once you know him, you'll understand that he's the perfect man for you. You've messed him around, upset him — you're a wicked girl, and you know what happens to wicked girls. They're kept locked up till they learn how to behave.'

Kristin began to shiver, and it wasn't only due to the fact that she was wet and cold, her clothes clinging to her. She couldn't believe what was happening to her. It was like something out of a Grimm's fairy tale. Clearly, Iris was mentally ill. No sane person would do something like this.

She looked around. There was a smell, a stale odour; dank. She wrinkled her nose and tried to breathe through her mouth. Maybe it was coming from the coats? Well, she certainly wasn't sniffing at them to see.

There were several shelves on

another wall; these were laden with what looked like piles of old newspapers. Apart from that, the space was empty. No toilet, as one would expect in a cloakroom; no washbasin. There was, however, a low three-legged stool in one corner. Kristin slumped down onto it, drawing her knees up to her chest and wrapping her arms tightly round them as she desperately tried to stop her violent shivering. For the fact was, she was growing colder and more clammy by the second. A single question hammered at her. If Iris was truly mad, as she feared, what exactly what would she be capable of?

She put that worry aside for the moment, however, and concentrated on a couple of other problems that had belatedly occurred to her. What if Richard didn't turn up? Or — oh God, what if he was colluding with his mother? How she going to get out? There were no windows — well, there wouldn't be in a cupboard, large or not.

There wasn't even any sort of air vent through which she could maybe call for help. They could keep her here as long as they wanted.

Her phone! What a fool. Why hadn't she thought of that earlier? She pulled it from her jeans pocket and had started to press the number for the police when she saw that there was no signal. Nothing. Zilch.

Real despair, the like of which she'd never before experienced, overcame her then. She was still terribly cold, and getting colder by the second. She began to rub vigorously at her bare arms in a vain attempt to instil some warmth into herself. She supposed she could put on one of the coats, but she couldn't bring herself to touch — let alone wear — anything that might belong to that mad woman. Or her son, come to that.

There was no way out that she could see. All she could do was wait for Richard to arrive, and hope he wasn't a full and willing partner in this scheme. If he was — ? No, she wouldn't even think that. She'd face it when she had to.

But it wasn't long before another problem arose. A far more urgent problem. She needed a toilet. Eventually, just as she was seriously considering urinating on the floor, she heard the front door open and Richard's voice calling, 'Mum; I'm home, Mum.'

Kristin leapt to her feet and ran to the door. 'Richard,' she shouted, 'it's me, Kristin!' She banged her fists on the door. All she could do was pray that Richard didn't share his mother's madness.

There was a moment's silence, and then, 'Kristin? Is that you? Where are you?'

'No, son, let her be.' It was Iris speaking from right outside the door.

'Mother, what have you done?'

'I've locked her in till she sees sense. Sees that you're the man for her.'

'Good grief! Get out of the way. For God's sake, are you completely mad?'

The door was yanked open and Richard stood there, white-faced and clearly shocked. Kristin all but fell through the doorway.

'Richard,' she gasped, 'thank goodness.'

'I'm so sorry,' he said. 'What can I say? She hasn't been herself for some time.'

'Don't make excuses for me,' Iris shouted. 'I know exactly what I'm doing.'

'No, Mother, you don't.' He looked back at Kristin, his expression one of abject pleading. 'Please — you won't report this, will you? To the police?'

'Richard, she's sick. She's been stalking me, scaring me. She even filled my tent with spiders.' She shuddered at the memory of the tiny creatures scurrying around her tent.

Richard's face paled until it was the colour of skimmed milk. 'I'll get help for her, I promise. A doctor. Please, just don't tell the police. They'll arrest her and it would surely kill her.'

By this time Iris had disappeared, gone into another room. Presumably in an attempt to escape retribution.

'It isn't simply a doctor she needs,' Kristin said. 'It's a psychiatrist.'

'I'll get one. I will; I promise.'

'Okay, but keep her away from me, because if ever I see her again . . . '

'I will. I will.'

'Right. Well, I'm going home now, back to my mother's.' And belatedly, that was all she wanted: to be with her mother, to be held in her arms, to be — safe.

'Yes, of course. I'll take you.'

★ ★ ★

Eve was appalled when Kristin related all that had happened to her. 'The crazy old witch,' she gasped.

'I know. Oh Mum, I was so scared. She looked totally mad.'

'I'll phone Grant, see what he thinks we should do.'

'No, please don't.'

But it was too late. Grant was already there, opening the front door with his key. 'You've given him a key?' Kristin asked in surprise.

'It seemed the right thing to do. He is going to be my husband.' Eve sounded defensive.

'Yes, of course. I'm sorry, I'm not criticising.'

Of course, Grant then had to be told what had happened. He was every bit as horrified as Eve had been. 'She should be locked up for everyone's safety,' he proclaimed. 'Are you okay, Kristin love?'

She nodded, even though some sort of delayed action was beginning to set in. She was shaking again, so much this time that it was all she could do to go on standing upright.

'Darling,' Eve murmured, 'it's all right; you're safe now.' She held her daughter close. Neither of them noticed Grant walking quietly out of the room. 'I won't let her near you again — or that wretched son of hers. Now, I'm

342

going to make a pot of tea.'

Kristin gave a watery smile. That was her mother's answer to everything: a nice cup of tea. All Kristin really wanted was a long, very hot bath. She was still extremely cold, although her clothes had almost dried.

Grant, however, had pre-empted her mother's intention and was already bringing in a tray of tea and biscuits. 'Here we are, ladies. I thought you might both need this. Me, I'm going to have a whisky.' He gave a mischievous smile.

Kristin had just taken a first cautious sip of the steaming hot liquid when she heard a car pulling up outside of the house. She didn't see Grant's stare at Eve or his mute signal to her to come with him out of the room. She was far too busy trying to work out who on earth it could be.

'I'll go,' said Eve and made her escape. Grant followed, hard on her heels.

Kristin felt too weary to even get up

from her chair. Her mother would deal with whoever it was.

'Hello,' she heard Eve softly saying. 'Did Grant call you?'

'Yes,' came the response.

Kristin couldn't believe her ears. It was Daniel. Why on earth would Grant call Daniel? He was the very last person she wanted to see, especially after the way in which they'd parted last time. Her initial instinct was to make a run for her bedroom, but as he was in the hallway, that course of action would be futile. It would have been too late anyway, for in the next second Daniel was striding into the sitting room.

'What do you want?' was Kristin's blunt question.

'I've already told you that. You,' was Daniel's equally blunt response.

'Well, you're out of luck. I'm not available.'

'My father's told me what happened. You clearly need looking after.' He had cocked his head to one side as he

344

studied her face. His eyes were gleaming silver.

'Oh, yes? Who by?'

'Me. Who else?'

'Why would you want to look after me?' She spoke slowly. There was a very strange look to him now.

'Did they hurt you?' he softly asked.

'No, just scared me. It wasn't Richard, it was his mother. It was all her. She had this crazy notion that scaring me and locking me up in some sort of cupboard-cum-cloakroom would make me turn to Richard. It was her stalking me too.'

Merely saying the words had tears springing into her eyes and, within another second, she was sobbing, her whole body shaking beneath the force of it. Good grief, she seemed to do nothing else but cry lately. She'd never been the weepy sort. It must be Daniel's fault; the effect he had on her. 'She's completely insane,' she wailed. 'I think she would have kept me there forever if she'd had her way.'

For a split second Daniel seemed paralysed, quite unable to move. But then in a single stride he was there, pulling her up from the chair, wrapping his arms about her, cradling her, gently rocking her and murmuring, 'There, there, sssh. You're safe now.'

But all that achieved was to make her cry even harder. 'I-I felt so-so alone,' she wept.

'Oh, my love, you're not alone. I'm here. I'll always be here.'

Kristin jerked back, to stare up at him, her eyes wide and tear drenched. 'What?'

'Don't you know? Haven't you guessed yet?' He smiled tenderly, stroking the damp tendrils of hair back from her face. 'I love you. I have from the second I saw you, striding across that field, so full of fury, and with such determination. Quite prepared to take the two of us on single-handedly. I wanted to kiss you, right there and then. I didn't, obviously.'

'You-you love me?' A wave of warmth

was flooding through her, despatching the bone-deep chill that she hadn't been able to shake off.

'Yes. I tried to tell you yesterday.'

She lifted a hand to stop him speaking. 'No, you said you wanted me. That's a completely different thing.'

'If you'd given me the chance I would have said I loved you.'

'Oh no,' she wailed. 'I've been through agonies.'

'You have?' He lifted an eyebrow. 'You could have fooled me then. You seemed so sure of yourself always.'

'Believe me, I wasn't. I felt at times as if I were dying. You can be so cold, so unfeeling.'

'Self-defence, that's all. You have an uncanny knack of stabbing a man right in the heart.' He grinned at her. 'But, just to get things straight — does all this mean you love me back?'

'Yes,' she whispered, shy all of a sudden.

'Well, about time!' He bent his head towards her; he was going to kiss her.

She had her lips raised to his when she remembered something. 'Hang on. Stop.' She pushed him away. 'Sophie. She told me you were practically engaged to her.'

'She what?' He snorted. 'Where the hell did she get that idea from?'

'You tell me.' She eyed him with suspicion.

'I have never, not by a single word or gesture, indicated such a thing.'

'Really?'

'Really.'

'Hmmm.'

'So with that cleared up — come here.' He reached for her again. 'There's something I want to do; need to do, actually — rather desperately.'

Kristin, for almost the first time since she'd met him, had absolutely no hesitation in doing exactly as he said.

He slid both arms around her, and, with eyes that gleamed, very, very slowly lowered his head to hers. He stopped an inch from her lips, by which time Kristin was so impatient that she put her own hand behind his head and yanked him down to her.

'Can't wait, huh?' he muttered.

'Not for another second,' she said, and they kissed, a kiss that went on — and on — and on.

THE END

We do hope that you have enjoyed reading this large print book.

Did you know that all of our titles are available for purchase?

We publish a wide range of high quality large print books including:
Romances, Mysteries, Classics
General Fiction
Non Fiction and Westerns

Special interest titles available in large print are:
The Little Oxford Dictionary
Music Book, Song Book
Hymn Book, Service Book

Also available from us courtesy of Oxford University Press:
Young Readers' Dictionary
(large print edition)
Young Readers' Thesaurus
(large print edition)

For further information or a free brochure, please contact us at:
Ulverscroft Large Print Books Ltd.,
The Green, Bradgate Road, Anstey,
Leicester, LE7 7FU, England.
Tel: (00 44) 0116 236 4325
Fax: (00 44) 0116 234 0205

ANGELA'S RETURN HOME

Margaret Mounsdon

It has been years since schoolteacher Angela Banks last saw Russ Stretton, but she remembers him only too well. She'd had a massive crush on him as a teenager, and now he was back in her life. But he's carrying considerable emotional baggage, including a five-year-old son, Mikey — not to mention a sophisticated French ex-wife, who seems intent on winning him back at all costs . . .

THE LOVING HEART

Christina Green

Lily Ross becomes nursemaid to young Mary, whose widowed father runs Frobisher's Emporium in their seaside village in Devon. She loves her job caring for Mary, a good-natured and spirited child. Although Matt, her fisherman friend, worries her with his insistent love that she cannot return, other things fill her life: Mary and her adventures, the strange flower lady — and her growing feelings for her employer, Mr Daniel. But as his nursemaid she must keep her feelings to herself, or risk losing her position . . .

THE FATAL FLAW

Anne Hewland

When a young woman wakes with no memory of her identity, she is told by Charles Buckler that he has rescued her from a vicious attack during her journey to Ridgeworth to become the intended bride of his distant cousin, Sir Ashton Buckler. An impostor has taken her place, however, and she must resume her rightful position. Who can Elinor believe? Is Charles all he seems? What happened to Sir Ashton's first wife — and why does someone at Ridgeworth resent her presence?